Ohj Beautiful

N E Ventre

This is a work of fiction. Names, characters, and events are fictitious. Any resemblance to actual persons, living or dead, is purely coincidental.

ISBN-13: 978-0692855256
ISBN-10: 0692855254

I love my family.

--T. K.

Ohj Beautiful

Chapter One

Ohj looked through the window at the crying man. Blood pooled on the laminate floor as fat drops fell from the man's head and nose.

"That's all the money we've got. If there was more, I'd give it to you." The curve of the man's spine rolled him into a hunch, as if he prayed to the intruder with a butcher knife.

As usual, Ohj arrived at the perfect time—the minute suspended between hope and the dawn of desperation. Ohj stood straight, arms relaxed at his sides as he analyzed the two kneeling humans. Ben and Lucille, parents of four, grandparents of eleven.

Ben started sobbing, giving up his pride along with his valuables. "You have it all. Please, let us go." His begging grew shrill with every word. "We won't tell anyone..., I swear to you..., we won't call...."

"Shut up already," the intruder yelled. "Damn. You're killin' my ears."

Ohj scanned the room. He didn't notice the neatness: lack of dust and vacuumed rug. He didn't care that the daisy curtains matched the yellow sofa to perfection. Several framed pictures of family trips crowded the coffee table. Those also failed to catch his eye. What Ohj did focus on was the plastic grocery bag near the doorway. It contained two fifty-year-old wedding bands, a coffee can full of pocket change, and a diamond bracelet worth much less at the local pawnshop.

The intruder—Ohj knew him as Scott—just broke the man's nose over this miserable amount. Today had turned out to be a waste of Scott's time. He'd targeted this house, despite the faded porch and old Corolla parked in the driveway, only because a friend had told him the elderly pair kept a wad of cash stashed inside. All their family vacations apparently convinced the neighbors they had money lying around.

Scott didn't bother to mask his face or even throw on a cap to hide the color of his greasy hair. Instead, to avoid getting caught, he planned to murder the couple. They would ultimately die over the fun-money they kept in a can for the grandkids.

Neither the man, the woman trembling beside him, nor Scott, knew that Ohj scrutinized each word, monitored every physical response. Not two feet away, Ohj stood where they thought the living room wall to be. Close enough to hear their hearts pounding, see the mist of sweat rising off their flannel pajamas. And Ohj could feel the whoosh of air as Scott shoved the five-inch blade into the older man's chest.

Posturing in shock, Ben grabbed at the knife. Lucille sucked in a lungful of air as the Bowie sunk in deeper, all the way to the handle.

With a spray of blood, Scott pulled the knife free from the bone and muscle. The old man crumpled, face down. Lucille screamed, releasing all the fear exploding in her lungs.

Ohj didn't move. He didn't rush forward to soften Ben's fall—prevent his head from hitting the floor. He didn't call for help. Although he hardly needed help in fighting off the scrawny punk who wielded the power of death over these two people as carelessly as if choosing between bottles or cans.

This murderer, with barely enough flesh to hang his clothes on, stood in front of a warrior. Had Ohj wanted, he could snap Scott's neck with one massive hand. If Scott saw Ohj, he'd be the one on his knees begging for mercy.

And if only Lucille could see Ohj—her knight in shining armor. All her fantasy champions combined into one beautiful hero, was actually at *her* house. Except Ohj didn't lift a finger to snap the murderer's neck. And was never inclined to do so. He didn't come here to help, at least not in the traditional sense. Ohj wasn't here to save her day; he was here to witness her death. And he would do an excellent job of it. Just for her.

She shook violently, her swollen fingers twisting at the front of her nightgown. "Oh, Ben, no. Dear God, please."

Ohj knew her knees wouldn't bear her weight on the cold floor for much longer.

"I know you got more crap than this." Scott waved the bloody knife in front of her face. "It's no

3

secret you have money. You better cough it up or you're gonna end up like gramps here. Is it in your mattress? Frozen in the ice cube bin...?"

She covered her mouth with her hand and shook her head.

"... in a shoe box behind all your other shit in the closet?" Scott grabbed a handful of hair at the crown of her head. "How 'bout we take a little walk 'round the house and you just point when we're close."

"There's no more," the woman whispered coarsely, scrambling to keep up with the wrenching.

"Cat got your tongue?" He tried to yank her to her feet. "Then, nod when we get warm. You can do that, right?"

She reached up, her fingers almost touching his hand, then her hand dropped. Her body sagged.

Scott held her up on her knees like a puppeteer. "What's up with you?" he yelled, gray strands sticking out between his knuckles. "Knock it off!"

After he let go of her, she remained kneeling. Her mouth popped open and closed as her torso began to convulse. She focused on a spot just beyond Scott's shoulder. As she swayed forward, Scott stepped back to give her room to hit the floor. She landed hard, face first, in the exact position as her husband. The married couple lay side by side, matched up perfectly, as if posed for an anniversary photo taken from behind.

Ohj nodded in approval: the best outcome in this situation. The two souls stood off by the door, holding hands. Still in their PJs, they watched the scene finish playing out. Each had their own guardian angel ready to escort them away. They weren't Ohj's concern anymore, so he shifted his attention back to Scott.

The junkie threw down his knife. "Shiiiiiit!" He balled up both fists and started kicking the woman's corpse. Ohj waited for him to finish.

"You stinking bitch!" He worked out his rage on her body, careful to avoid bloodying his shoes in the red puddle spreading out from under Ben. "Bitch, bitch, you fucking bitch...." He started to sweat as each kick lifted her corpse off the floor.

Stopping abruptly, he jerked off his gloves with his teeth. Hands free, he unzipped his pants.

Ohj groaned, hoping Scott wasn't going to make them all watch him masturbate over the bodies. It wouldn't be the first time. What things people did when they thought no one watched, never surprised him. He spared a quick glance at the confused souls, thinking that now would be a good time for their guardians to lead them away.

Instead, Scott started urinating, aiming first at one body, then the other, running his piss up and down their prone backs. The hot scent of urine and spring-fresh, fabric softener floated into the air. After shaking off, he zipped, re-gloved, grabbed his grocery bag, and ran out the door for a quick escape. Ohj glanced at the sickly yellow pool mingling with blood. Probably not enough DNA to nail him for the crime. Or maybe there was: didn't matter to him either way.

With a head-pivot to the right, he gave up his visual of the room. He turned his back on the large window as it darkened on the bodies.

His sparse witness room was quiet with the window shut. Its four white walls and one light hanging from the ceiling had all the charm of a freshly painted prison cell. Nothing to distract him from the action in the window. Some witnesses decorated their rooms as if expecting company: with colorful murals, or a sofa set on a plush rug. He'd even seen one covered with dolphins, of all things. Dolphins swimming on the ceiling, frolicking around the walls and floors—sweet, rubbery smiles keeping the witness company.

Not all witness' rooms were created equal. Ohj worked one of the darker rooms: a real-time display of all the horrible things that humans do to one another.

He sat down at a lone desk wedged in the corner, next to his old fighting sword. This account was an easy one, but his report on Scott wouldn't be flattering. He'd witnessed for Scott before, always when he needed drug money. In Scott's defense, if Ohj had cared to defend him, he might have been a nice boy once. Perhaps a boy scout who had volunteered to mow lawns for little old ladies. But now he just peed on them. For Ohj, that trumped the possibility that ten years earlier he might have mowed her lawn for free. But again, defending Scott wasn't his job—or his problem.

After writing up the account, down to the smallest detail, Ohj tossed the report onto Scott's growing stack. Judging by his skin pallor and jitters, he'd see him again soon enough.

The room had two doors. Ohj took the one leading to a small antechamber where a soft glow illuminated a table. Set in the middle, next to a stack of thick, white towels, was a large basin of carved stone. Except for his sword, the carving on the bowl was the only decoration he tolerated: battle scenes from his past, cut into the gray rock to expose white, flecked granite. Remembering his battle days helped him keep his edge. He had to stay grounded, before he too started decorating in dolphin-chic.

Carefully, he peeled off his shirt to begin the process of washing away contamination. The dirt wasn't physical—he hadn't left his room to pick up any. Instead, the dirt was spiritual; he could feel it, and even smell it. The remnants clung to him: the couple's pungent murder, blended with Scott's addiction, hatred and evil. It was as contaminating as if Scott had used Ohj's sleeve to wipe off the knife.

Ohj dipped both hands into the bowl and scooped up fresh water infused with pressed mint. He inhaled deeply to replace the stench in his nostrils before splashing his face. Dipping each arm in up to the elbow, he let the water rinse away the cruelty, then kicked off his pants. He drenched a cloth and squeezed it over his abdomen and legs until a stream ran down to the stone under his feet. Eventually, his skin began to glow again.

Ohj was clean.

He pronounced his name, "oh," softly, as if coming to a sudden understanding. It didn't burden the tongue with too many syllables or consonants. Simple—just how he liked it.

Wet towels and dirty clothes remained untouched on the floor after drying; to avoid re-contamination. Across the room lay a fresh set: shoes, pants, and long-sleeved shirt, all made from a light woven cloth. The same clothes he'd worn for half a millennium, ever since he'd become a heavenly witness.

He walked down a hall painted in soothing blues; the route that led to the pools. He had time: as much as he cared to take. Other witness rooms surrounded him on both sides. The chambers were ironically quiet, almost peaceful, from outside in the hallway. Open any one of those doors and screams of terror could shatter the tranquil mood. Ohj never cared to test a knob. He didn't need access to more torture and death. He preferred quiet, and the peaceful transition of the hallway.

The baths were in a cavernous room: high walls and arched ceiling carved from slabs of swirling marble. Five wading pools, specifically for the witnesses, were set up in Roman style, with seats molded into the sides. Ohj yanked his shirt over his shoulders and dropped his pants. A few witnesses were already inside, soaking up the water and enjoying time before their next job. He grabbed a towel and waded into the closest pool, a medium-sized rectangle with a long seat flanking each side.

The other witnesses didn't spare so much as a glance. In the small group gathered, no one talked, shared deep dark secrets, or gave advice. Nor did anyone gossip about their latest job. Most of the time, they didn't bother themselves to make eye contact, let alone offer a good-day. No offense intended or expected. The social distance made it easy on each other. Softer witnesses, like the ones who specialized in births and happy events, usually mingled with humans and guardians. Most of this group present were of the hardcore variety, capable of absorbing large amounts of cruelty, only to return the following day for more.

Ohj, for one, handled the savagery of his job just fine. All he needed was a little minty water to splash in his eyes afterwards.

He sat down across from a witness with skin that shined gold and hair that hung down in matted ropes, like an un-bathed Viking's. Terrifying—if he weren't so pretty. The witness made up for his chiseled cheeks and perfect nose by looking like he wanted to split open someone's skull. Beauty and beast in one being.

Violets skimmed the top, scenting the warm water. Ohj ran wet hands over his hair to keep stragglers off his face. He turned his chin toward the skylights that let in the sun that nourished them all. Ohj couldn't complain. He had the form of a human, but without the same needs. Right this second, he didn't have one need unmet: one itch to scratch. Eyes closed, he soaked up the heat that radiated just for him, filling him with rapturous contentment. Frustration, anger, or any undesirable thought simply melted away beneath the healing beams.

A small wave hit his chest and sloshed over the edge. He cracked an eyelid to see another being stepping into his pool. The witnesses soaking in the other pools glanced over at the guardian angel, a rare visitor to the pools. Their curiosity lasted only as long as it took for them to close their eyes again. Ohj continued to stare at the angel bobbing next to the Viking. The Viking dwarfed the guardian, whose curlicues of blonde hair dangled over blue eyes blinking with emotion. It was like taking a bath with a baby doll.

The baby doll nodded at him. "Just here to enjoy the peace and quiet."

The Viking snorted and climbed out.

Despite a strong urge to jump out along with the Viking, Ohj hesitated. Sharing a pool with a guardian was unsettling, but he wasn't sure if bolting out would be rude. His next thought was irritation: that this creature drove him to consider etiquette. He tried to focus on the light above, drawing more healing waves into his mind to dissolve his annoyance.

A faint smile on his Cupid's bow lips, the guardian rocked from side to side as if keeping time to his own mental choir.

The top of Ohj's head grew hot from the light while he still frowned at the guardian across from him. He silently counted to six, the highest number he could stand, then got out. "Have to go—enjoy your stay...."

If the guardian replied, Ohj didn't hear; too busy throwing on his clothes. His thoughts were back on work. A scheduled court hearing, where a decade's worth of account books waited for him.

Outside, a brilliant blue sky greeted him as he headed for the park in front of the courthouse. Beyond a hill thick with trees, a massive lake shimmered. He liked to wait right at the water's edge, until it was time for his cases to begin. The daily trek was only a short walk. A distance marred by any number of guardians, who always attempted to be pleasant.

"Beautiful day." The guardian, a female in a blue gown, greeted him with a lovely smile.

Ohj dipped his head in a slight nod. He never smiled, so not to encourage a conversation, or worse—a hug. Looking straight ahead to avoid eye contact with others he passed, he marched over to his favorite area.

Several cushioned benches were scattered close by, which he left for the guardians to fight over. His spot was an indentation in the hill, pliable as foam and cushioned with velvety grass.

He dropped down on the warmed velvet, dotted with blue wildflowers that hop-scotched their way to the water. Geese and swans glided along on the glittering lake, their paddling creating a soft wave that lapped at the edge of the grass. Every so often, a flying fish jumped up into the air before arching back in a graceful splash. Long legs stretched out in front of him, Ohj lifted his face to the light to absorb more heat, finishing the job he'd started in the pool. Under the unfiltered, concentrated light, his forearms and hands shined. Each individual cell ignited until his skin gleamed. When he began to tingle from the warmth, he closed his eyes and let his entire body recharge.

He felt good: a good day's work behind him, and a better day in court ahead. Thankfully, the sky had not one cloud to interrupt its brilliant blue pallet. The sun was warm, never scorching, though Ohj liked it hot. The more heat beating down, the more energy to absorb. If he had control over the thermostat, he'd set it on broil.

He needed this strength today. Some trials meant more to him than others. This was one of those he'd hungered for. He had a dozen written accounts on Ronald, who had tortured, raped, and then killed twelve women. Each episode read worse than the previous, as Ronald's needs became more insatiable. At first, the sessions took only hours. Eventually they lengthened into days. By the last victim, even Ohj wanted to look away.

But he didn't so much as blink an eye or hum a tune to drown out the screams; so not to miss even the tiniest of details.

Today Ronald was going to court. As Ohj's job designated, he'd be there as the only witness. Ohj would testify on Ronald's extreme cruelty; how he savored the victims' agony. Because of Ohj's testimony, along with the twelve, detailed accounts he brought, Ronald would be sent away to a very unpleasant eternity. Ohj had been looking forward to this day ever since the first time he'd opened his window to find Ronald smiling, stun gun in hand.

A shock of color appeared beside him. Lazily, Ohj turned his head to look.

"Hear you're in my courtroom today." The being in a deep royal blue robe settled down next to Ohj and leaned forward, elbows on his knees.

Ohj went back to the sun. "Yeah. Expect a long afternoon. I saved up years for this one."

"That's what I figured. Unlike you, I dread these cases. They make it hard for me to keep my sense of humor."

Ohj called this friend "Red" because of one distinctive tomato-orange gown he used to wear. Red ruled over this country court. Inside the courtroom and out he always wore a robe, in colors that rarely matched the gravity of the occasion. The colors were always in the brightest shades possible, as if the judge wasn't visible enough behind his dais. That left Ohj to figure that Red just liked wearing gaudy robes.

Red shook out a billowing blue sleeve. "Your cases suck the life outta me like nothing else can, but you come out lit up brighter than a supernova."

"Someone has to do it. I don't know why, but there's never a line of volunteers to take my place in my witness room."

"Can't say I blame 'em. By the time you're at the scene, all anyone can do is watch the slicing and dicing, hoping it ends soon."

They stared ahead, watching a guardian whose arms and neck were covered in tattoos. The shine from his skin radiated through the ink, creating a stained-glass glow that shined up onto his face. When the guardian caught sight of Red, a smile flashed, and his step picked up. Ohj tensed. When the guardian got closer, his eyes fell on Ohj. He shifted, waved at Red, then continued his original path.

Ohj didn't dislike guardians. Sometimes they worked together in the sense that Ohj remained at the scene while the guardians escorted a soul away. But frequently by the time the guardians arrived, he was already done with the event and moving on to the next. Never did the guardians intervene, at least not in any of Ohj's cases: lost causes with terrible endings. The guardians didn't even stay to watch those last few horrible moments. That puzzled Ohj. They were spectacular and powerful beings, though not nearly as impressive as he. Still, to remain with their beloved people through a shocking death, should be just as easy for them.

Maybe they couldn't. Lucky for the humans, Ohj could.

Red acknowledged two others sitting on a bench a few yards away. "My job's not always stress-free, but at least it's pleasant at times," he said, turning back to Ohj. "Recently, I had this wonderful child in the courtroom. Looked about ten years old in her little hat and white gloves, like she was sitting in a pew at Sunday school. Not one complaint against her—a perfect life. And yet she was ninety-two when she died: plenty of time to do some damage."

"That just means someone didn't do their job. You should have called me; I would have found something."

They sat a moment, thinking about innocence, hats, and gloves. Then Red sighed. "So, is there gonna be a lot of slicing and dicing today?"

Ohj stood up and stretched his arms high above him. Muscles rippled underneath his shirt. "You might want to call in sick for this one."

"I had my suspicions as soon as I noticed your good mood." Red stood up a foot shorter, counting the slouch. "Let's get this over with."

They zigzagged in and around the light crowd. Red slowed down by the time they got to the massive courtroom steps. Concentrating on the sun that warmed his back, Ohj felt energetic enough to take them in twos, leaving Red behind.

As Ohj approached the courthouse, he saw a couple of large soldiers blocking the entrance. The soldiers had a grip on a guardian, pushing him down to the ground. Clashes were so rare, one oblivious guardian after another tried to make their way straight through the scene. A soldier, sword at her hip, started pushing back those who got too close. The pedestrians eventually gave the soldiers their distance. After recognizing that one of their own was held down by the armed soldiers, a crowd formed. Deep frowns altered their normally serene expressions.

Ohj wasn't worried about the guardian's well-being. The fact that the soldiers' swords remained sheathed at their sides seemed a good sign this wasn't serious.

Red caught up to him. "I was afraid of this. But knew it was coming."

When he finally got a look at the guardian, Ohj recognized him. This guardian pushed all the boundaries of good taste, picking outrageous clothes from random periods of time. But other than dressing criminally bad, there wasn't much trouble he could get into.

The scuffle turned messy. The guardian, though no match for the soldiers, started to shout and fight. By the time the soldiers got control, yanking the guardian back up to his feet, he was in restraints. Chains wound around his wrists, binding his hands behind him.

"What a sad day." Red looked away from the guardian. "Maybe I should postpone today's cases. What do you think? This is disturbing—will it taint your testimony?"

Ohj lifted an eyebrow. "Of all things, why would this disturb me?"

Two guardians turned sharply to him. He lowered his voice and leaned towards Red. "This has nothing to do with my case. We all have work to do. Let's not forget our responsibilities because one guardian did something stupid."

A guardian approached Red. "Can't you do something to help him?"

"I'm sure he'll be fine." Red put a hand on her arm. "Let's just see what the judgment is. No need to worry yet."

The guardian turned her attention back to the soldiers. When they led their detainee away, she trailed behind out of support.

Once the way to the courtroom cleared, Ohj was the first to stride through the double-wide doors. All others slowly fell in behind.

Guardians and witnesses filled stacked rows of benches that formed the descending half-circle facing the judge's platform. The walls soared thirty feet high, with no ceiling to restrain them. Despite the openness, no sounds invaded the room from the park: just quiet, open sky above. Eight walls leaned in against each other, and were painted not with color, but with molded pictures of humanity. Each three-dimensional replica was pulled from history, becoming a seamless part of the whole chamber.

Red walked up a platform of five, marbled steps. They narrowed successively in pyramid fashion, until they reached a matching podium. He rested his hand on a boulder-thick, gold tome. Ohj stood in front, slightly to the side. He looked straight ahead, his arms bearing the weight of Ronald's twelve condemning books.

A few feet away from Ohj stood Ronald's guardian, there to tell of all the good deeds Ronald had done in the years before Ohj had met him. Unfortunately for Ronald, Ohj had met him at fifteen.

Ohj ignored this guardian—his testimony was redundant, a waste of the court's time. And when his turn came, Ohj would read the accounts as he always did: without any emotion. The crimes spoke for themselves: no dramatics necessary. Ronald also would get a chance to defend himself before sentencing. Usually after Ohj testified, people didn't bother with their side of the story.

A slight hum floated overhead. Ohj tuned into it as it began to grow, becoming palpable, warm. Once the room grew brighter, the crowd quieted.

Red nodded, motioning it was time to start. "Bring in the first defendant."

Two guards escorted Ronald. His gait was slow, weighed down by thick chains that drooped between his forearms and wrists. Head down, he shook, just like his victims did in their last moments of life: shaking with terror, agony.... The guards dragged Ronald to a spot in front of Red's platform. After they let go of his arms, the weight of the chains pulled him to the ground with a clang. This quivering human was unrecognizable to Ohj.

"Your name." Red's order cut through the rustling.

Face to his knees, Ronald whispered inaudibly. He gave a throaty cough and tried again, but his voice cracked.

Red looked down at his book, then back at the man crumpled on the marble floor. "Why are you here in chains? What crimes are you charged with?" Instead of waiting for an answer from Ronald, who still faced the floor, he looked at Ohj and lifted a hand for him to begin.

Ohj stepped forward and spoke clearly enough for everyone to hear, "I have witnessed many crimes committed by Ronald Bass, and I will give the court my testimony." He swung all the books to one arm and with his free hand, opened book one to page one. Ronald's first account, when he raped a seventeen-year-old girl from his high school, twice, before strangling her with the chain from his bike lock.

Before Ohj could take a breath to begin, someone walked up the aisle. He didn't hear them but couldn't miss the commotion from the crowd. The rustling started at the back and rippled forward, as if someone were bending through a pack of cards. Annoyed by the interruption, Ohj turned around and stared openly. A being strode to the front, not stopping until he stood right beside Ohj.

Half-foot taller, he wore his gold hair cropped short, and his bronze skin radiated such an intense heat it warmed Ohj's entire left side. His eyes had the tenderness of a guardian, but also carried the steel necessary to witness. A flash of déjà vu struck Ohj: he'd fought side by side with this enormous creature on the battlefield. During battle, he'd been grateful to have him nearby. Instincts warned him that this wasn't a good time to get reacquainted.

Currently, the being worked as a High Witness, one of a rare few, and very close to the Throne. The High Witness glanced at Ohj, his expression softening for a moment, then he faced Red. "I'd like to give my testimony on Ronald first. The witness that I bear will exonerate him of all crimes."

Ohj almost dropped his books.

Ronald stopped sobbing. He tried to stand, but under the weight of the lead chains, could only strain his neck. The shock on Ronald's face—blood drained and features slack—mirrored Ohj's.

Chapter Two

Red's gaze never strayed from the High Witness. "Continue."

The crowd ahhed as the light above radiated. Ohj closed his eyes and shook his head. Was he getting too cocky, or had it just been so long that he'd forgotten this possibility? He ached, knowing what was coming, and fought a screaming urge to wrestle this massive being out of the courtroom. Little chance he'd win anyway.

"Ronald begged forgiveness for the terrible crimes he committed...." The new witness had a bottomless voice, calmly launching the words. "... He showed consistent remorse and humility for the remainder of his days...."

No, no, no..., Ohj chanted mentally, trying to block his ears from the assault.

"...He cast off his old nature and wore a cloak of mercy and charity. While paying restitution on earth, he demonstrated many Christian acts in his remaining years; more than most humans do in a lifetime. I looked into his heart myself and saw only benevolence." The light overhead grew too bright, forcing all eyes downward. The High Witness paused for a breath. "I'm here with the request that he be set free."

The crowd began tapping their feet in anticipation of Red's decision. The drumming vibrated the walls, then bounced back inward to pressurize the room.

Ohj took a step forward to regain Red's attention. He raised his arm, trying to quiet the crowd. When that failed, he addressed Red directly, shouting over the commotion.

"Despite the last testimony, I would still like to give my own," he hollered to Red. "Not to dispute the argument that Ronald lived his last few years of life with remorse, but the depravity of his crimes merit special consideration. They should be accounted for." He added emphasis to the words, *depravity* and *crimes,* yelling them a little louder than the rest. "With great respect intended to the defense," He gave the High Witness a short nod. "It's the least the court can do."

Ohj doubted he had a fighting chance, but he had to try. The horrendous acts of cruelty still played in his mind. The victims' screams filled his ears as if they lay bleeding at his feet in the courtroom. He'd written the details in his books but could recite them from memory; from the first victim, to the last, begging for her life until she could no longer speak.

After hearing these terrible crimes, the court couldn't accept Ronald's release so passively. As Red considered Ohj's request, the crowd went quiet, sucking up all the air. Ohj's head began to pound from the switchbacks.

Red looked to the High Witness for direction. The High Witness bowed his head in consent. Red then nodded at Ohj to continue.

Ronald began crying again. He knew what he had done. He knew he deserved the worst punishment imaginable.

Ohj took a deep breath in preparation for a strong reading. This testimony was going to get all he had, every dramatic tool he owned and never used. Again, he opened the first book to page one. The page was blank. He flipped to the next page, and the next. His words were gone. He turned the stack over in his arms to sift through the last book, the thickest. Seventy-one hours of terror vanished as if they had never occurred.

As he searched the books, the significance squeezed his heart and lungs. His memory did him no good if the words weren't written down.

After a few more painful seconds, Ohj met Red's eyes. "I have nothing to add."

The crowd remained silent, but their feet started thrumming, waiting for Red's next words.

"Ronald Bass, you may go in peace."

Red nodded to the guards. They stepped forward and unchained Ronald. After the chains fell off, the prisoner bounced upwards, then he dropped back down, landing on top of the metal pile, his face buried in his hands.

The roar shook the room. Stomping rocked the floor beneath the guardians' feet. Ohj stood a moment, eyes shut, before turning to the crowd. He searched the faces, hoping to find at least one shouting in protest. But these faces all smiled. Not tight, polite smiles, but crazed, open-mouthed grins. All because the court set a murderer free. The only outrage in the room was his. Ohj frowned at the party that rewarded a monster for his terrible crimes.

Not even his old friend seemed to comprehend what just happened. At his podium, Red still drank in the magnificence of the High Witness. No one appreciated what an injustice this was, because no one else had witnessed the atrocity. They didn't have a clue—and they never would; the deeds were erased.

Ohj turned away from the look of delight on Red's face. As he pushed his way to the door, several congratulatory hands clapped him on the back, propelling him forward. He needed to get out fast and get his emotions back under control. Mostly, he wanted to escape.

A hand on his shoulder stopped him outside on the steps. It took an effort not to pull away from the blue sleeve.

"Every soul is worth saving, Ohj."

Ohj straightened his spine. His own job wasn't to judge; technically, he had no right. He rearranged his facial expression before turning to his friend. Not able to force a smile, he did manage less of a sneer. "Just caught me off guard."

"Come back inside. Talk with Ronald—it'll do you good."

That suggestion did make Ohj smile: a real one, wide enough to bare all his teeth.

Yes, he would love to chat with Ronald—only not in front of so many spectators.

"No. My afternoon is suddenly free. I'm going to get extra work done."

Red gave a quick nod and spun around. He ran up the stairs to rejoin the celebration. When the door opened, shouts of the fanfare slipped into the street. Guardians from the park turned their heads and started to make their way towards the joy, like zombies in search of brains. Soon the courthouse would get too confined and the riot of happiness would ooze out onto the streets.

Ohj walked fast to get out of its path.

He headed towards his workroom, wishing he hadn't told Red he was going to work. Lying wasn't part of his make-up; now he had no choice but do just that—work.

His pulse beat in his ears as he walked. Not one of Ronald's victims' guardians shouted out today on behalf of the women. Where were those angels? Their absence betrayed the very creatures they loved so blindly. Maybe if they had spoken up, all twelve of them storming the court, they could've gotten justice. He shot glances at the angels passing him, daring them to wish him happiness, but none of them looked at him. They all focused on the courthouse and the frenzy on the steps.

The witness room was too small to contain his restlessness; he needed to pace off his anger. After a few short stomps around the room, he sat down and grabbed his last report off the floor. From the corner of his eye the silhouette of his window hovered, encircled by a faint light. An event needed his witness. He ignored it.

Shuffling and sloshing from his antechamber let him know he wasn't the only one in his quarters. His contaminated clothes were being replaced with a clean set, always left folded neatly on a chair. Fresh water poured into his bowl, the floor dried. Soon the room would be immaculate. The process usually occurred when he wasn't there, so not to distract him. The mix-up was caused by Ronald's premature finale.

A few times he glanced sideways, his eyes drawn to the hazy film of his window. The event would wait, he knew. He went back to his report, rereading it. His mind flashed lucid images for him, as if he witnessed Scott murder the elderly couple that instant—again.

And again.

He tossed the book and intended to head to the pools: the last place he'd find a celebration. But before he got two steps, the window began humming. He turned, half debating whether to make a run for it.

The window glowed hot, pulling him towards it despite himself. A satiating warmth always pulsated while it was open, drawing him into the unobstructed and panoramic view. The space took up the entire fourth wall of the room, spanning wider than he could reach with outstretched fingertips. He crossed the room and stood in front; shoulders back, arms down.

As the scene brightened, he scanned it carefully.

A boy, Garrett, ten years old, was tied to a kitchen table. Spasms shook his body.

"Are you kidding me?" Ohj hissed, recognizing the kitchen immediately: Wayne's kitchen. He started to turn. "I'm not in the mood for this."

While he considered the door to the hallway, the event continued, apparent by the boy's whimpers of fear. Shaking his head, Ohj forced himself back to the scene. He straightened his posture and took in the spectacle.

Foil covered the curtained window over the sink. Another window, over the breakfast nook, was concealed by a thick sheet of vinyl upholstery material. No natural light entered the room. The table was dragged into the middle of the kitchen and the chairs were stacked in Wayne's bedroom across the hall. Four pieces of weathered rope pulled the boy's extremities in the direction of each table leg. His hands and feet had started turning blue from the lack of circulation. A larger boy wouldn't have fit on the tabletop, but Garrett was small for his age.

The boy's clothes were cut, the Scratch lines going through to his skin. A flap of his jeans fell away a few inches above his knee, exposing a black birthmark. The mark, large and oddly square, seeped red from a nick. On the floor next to him lay the torn carcass of the terrier he'd followed into the house. Tufts of dog hair stuck to the puddles of blood as if it were glue.

Ohj had witnessed for Wayne three times before. He wasn't sure whose bad luck, his or Wayne's, that he was here again now. He concentrated on Wayne, clearing his mind of his last trial, so not to be distracted by own his emotions. A familiar stench engulfed the room. Before he'd arrived, the kitchen must have been crammed with demons. Rather than face Ohj, they'd left their prize behind, missing out on the entertainment.

Dazed, Garrett cried. The cuts on his stomach and legs, though painful, were minor: little more than scratches. Those early wounds weren't examples of what lay ahead for boy. Smiling, Wayne approached the table, hiding something behind his back. The gardening shears were easy enough for Ohj to spot.

Wayne leaned over the boy. "Wanna see what I got?" He shoved the open blades into Garrett's face. "Gotch yer nose," he said, pretending to snap off the tip. The boy cried out.

"I'm kidding." Wayne laughed as he dragged the shears along the wood towards the boy's feet. The scraping vibrated the table, making Garrett jump.

Ohj wanted this over—now. He leaned forward to see every corner of the kitchen, hoping to find the boy's guardian. He found no guardian, which meant no hope. Garrett wasn't going to get a last-minute reprieve. He blew out a lungful of air. The window trembled, almost undetectably.

Holding the shears midair, Wayne's head lifted.

Ohj caught his breath and held it as Wayne's eyes flicked around, then straight through him, settling on a spot just off his right shoulder. Frozen, they faced each other; one not seeing the other. After another minute, Wayne scratched his jaw and let his gaze fall.

Ohj shook his head at his own sloppy work. If he couldn't show restraint, then he shouldn't have opened the window. He lifted an arm to close it. He'd still have to finish the event, every second of it, but only after his head was on straight.

"You know—I don't like boys. I ain't no queer. What I really wanted was a little girl."

Those words made Ohj pause. He marveled at how Wayne came up with such pain—how, even by accident, he was so good at damaging others. Garrett was well familiar with the sentiment: *I wanted a girl.* A frequent observation by the boy's mother. That reminder of his mother's disappointment would strike

26

the boy's heart as precisely as if Wayne had used a scalpel.

Wayne picked up a pair of pliers. "Yeah, I only like girls."

Anticipating Wayne's intent, Ohj's breathing quickened. He felt minimal relief when Wayne moved past the boy's pants, taking the device instead to Garrett's face.

The boy's mouth was already open in fear, so Wayne easily jammed the pliers inside. The abuser held Garrett's jaw immobile with his other hand as he clamped the pliers around the boy's tongue. "I don't want you tellin' anyone about this. Don't want to get called no queer." He pulled the boys tongue out past his lips, and then reached for a pair of utility scissors. As the cold blades began to tighten, Garrett's screamed.

"STOP." Ohj shouted from behind his window.

The window billowed outward, before shifting back into place. Ohj grit his teeth to keep his mouth shut.

Wayne dropped the scissors and ran over to the window. He pushed his head underneath the vinyl sheet to look out.

Ohj looked behind also, taking his eyes off the scene for the second time. His room was quiet, and no sounds came from his antechamber.

In the kitchen, Wayne still crouched behind the curtain, stretching his neck to see into the corners of the yard and below the window.

Ohj rolled his head around and shook out his arms to decompress. A few tiny flecks of silver floated to the floor. Never had he lost it before—never came close. *This* he found disturbing.

He'd finish this session for Wayne, then wait until he regained complete composure to do another. Without objectivity, he was useless, worse—dangerous. Careful to face away, he took a slow breath, dropped his hands to his sides, and began to take in the scene as if the window had just opened: boy on table, dog on floor, Wayne fidgeting behind a vinyl curtain.

A little paler, Wayne went back to the table. Ohj relaxed a bit, hoping the interruption scared him enough to stop. This was Wayne's chance to turn the situation around, maybe even get redemption. Crazier things had happened that day.

But Wayne wasn't interested in the opportunity for a new beginning. He picked up the scissors and set them on Garrett's leg. The boy's shaking made the clippers bounce.

"Hey, look at that—they can dance." Wayne said with a smile.

"Come on, you're done now," Ohj whispered. He scratched at his neck, freeing more silver flecks into the air. Wayne resumed his pose, grasping the boy's jaw.

"Mommy, mommy...." Garrett cried for the only protector he knew.

A sad pick, Ohj thought.

Garrett screamed hoarsely, as Wayne closed in.

"NO!" Ohj shoved at the window in front of him with both hands. The motion rippled through the window in a burst, knocking Wayne backward. His heels landed in dog's blood then slipped up from underneath him. For a fraction, he was airborne. The scissors scratched Garrett's arm as they too flew up.

28

Wayne landed flat on his back, the scissors following, point down in his chest.

Wayne convulsed on the floor, eyes blinking. His blood pumped out and around the blades, soaking his Hurley t-shirt.

Ohj held his hands up in the air and pressed his lips together. He now had a damaged pedophile and a boy tied to a table in his room. This would be tough to explain, especially today. Not to mention: what if the boy couldn't get himself off the table? The dog obviously wouldn't run for help.

Maybe Wayne had enough life in him to drag himself to the phone? Ohj checked: the blades had landed with amazing precision, sliding between two ribs to nick his heart. Wayne had quit moving altogether and was now undoubtedly headed to confront him in Red's court—another scenario Ohj didn't want to think about.

He went to his antechamber to double-check that no one still cleaned, then looked out the door, down both lengths of the corridor, to make sure nobody heard the scene from the hallway. The boy started crying as Ohj contemplated what to do next.

New movement in the window caught his eye. The boy's guardian appeared. Usually apathetic to the guardians, Ohj had never appreciated their presence. He appreciated it now.

The guardian, a male in jeans and gray hoodie, walked a full circle around the room. He stepped over Wayne's body to get to the boy. When he put his hand on Garrett's forehead, the boy instantly calmed. The guardian stroked the boy's hair, cooling his sweat-dampened brow, until Garrett fell into a comforted sleep. The guardian looked through the window at

Ohj, then around the room again appearing neither happy nor relieved that his boy just escaped a terrible death.

Ohj figured the guardian took extra time soothing the boy to figure out what had happened. He, too, tried to think: tossing around various excuses. His problem was—there wasn't one explanation he was ready to admit to. So, when he caught the guardian's eye again, he gave an exaggerated shrug.

The guardian nodded. He loosened Garrett's bindings, even slipping one wrist out from the rope. He plugged an old phone back into its wall jack, and stood over the boy, waiting for him to wake up.

Ohj closed the window and dropped to the ground. The ordeal was over. Now all that was left to do was wait for the soldiers to come pounding on his door. Maybe the same couple who had just chained up the guardian on the court steps. They were probably still close by. The ground around him sparkled with the silver flecks that normally dusted his skin. It occurred to him that the soldiers would find him cowering on the floor, in his own filth.

He got up and went into the antechamber to purify for their arrival. The room was quiet and fresh smelling. He stripped down and shoved his face into the water. Before coming back up, he rubbed his eyes and cheeks. Instead of dripping the washcloth over his body, he brushed, to knock off any loose cells. He then dressed in his whites, stood a foot from the door, and waited.

There wouldn't be a kicking and screaming scene when they came. No chains necessary, and no grand production for the crowd. His chin would be high, and he'd face his due punishment with honor.

Countless seconds turned to several minutes, then hours, as Ohj waited in the middle of the room. Despite his lack of resistance, no one came to take him away. He moved off his spot and opened the door. He gave the soldiers a count of one hundred, and then went home.

He concentrated on the feel of his feet hitting the walkway. Large leafed trees rained flower petals. They floated around him in pink tufts, landing at his shoes and in his hair. He passed one house where beautiful music filled his ears with a symphony of harmonized cellos and guitars. The music followed him, forcing him to pick up his pace.

The walk to his house was long. By the time he opened the door to his small box of a home, he was well out of view of neighbors, let alone casual strollers. He shook the petals off his head. The absence of color inside soothed his eyes, while the lack of clutter soothed his mind. Large open windows invited a breeze to flow through and pick up the scent of mint and lemon from scattered bowls. The fragrance swirled around him as he went from window to window, shutting each one. Then he sat on the floor and leaned against the door.

Remain objective and maintain composure were crucial dictates of witnessing. Intervening was at the top of the list of *what not to do*. Might even be #1. In fact, he wasn't sure if there was a #2, let alone a #3.

What he just did in Wayne's kitchen disqualified him: he could no longer witness. Nor did he have the right to face anyone in court. That he got away with it so far, just compounded his crime. He now harbored a criminal—himself.

31

Before, with his stoicism and professional passivity, he was the best. Others were trained to follow his perfect lead. But now that he intervened, other witnesses might be tempted in their own moment of weakness, ruining a perfect system. He might have just started a coup.

He had to do the honorable thing: turn himself in, not just go along peacefully after they caught him lurking around. As he sat on the floor, he debated when and how to do the honorable. Quietly surrendering to Red might be the least humiliating option. Yet the idea didn't flood him with relief.

His job would've been easier if the soldiers had dragged him off at work.

After a few hours, he went to lie down on his bed. He dropped down on his cot and stared at a boarded window. He didn't like to eat, so kept no food in the house. Lack of food left him with one less option to keep him occupied as he waited for a bolt of inspiration.

He wondered what happened when the boy's guardian got him home safe. And hoped the boy went home to a mother so relieved he was alive, and with all his limbs intact, that she began to cherish him. If anyone earned a few years of love, Garrett did.

That boy deserved a second chance at happiness. Regardless of his own crime, he wouldn't apologize to the court for giving the boy that. For that, he wasn't sorry. He thought about his countless cases, the children and adults before Garrett, where he carried out his job to perfection. Too many to count. Garret was just one case.

Before today, he held an amazing record. He was the best. A shame for humanity to lose him after one lapse. To quit now would be a disservice. By abandoning his post, he could actually worsen the damage on a grander level.

The weight fell from his shoulders once he made his decision; he would keep his mouth shut and get back to the job he was so good at. He stood up and checked if the decision stuck. Even standing, the decision felt good. He walked towards the door. Still felt fine.

Confident he was right, he opened the door.

The walk back went faster, his steps lighter. Only positive vibrations filled the air—it was a normal day. The sun welcomed him as he dropped onto the grassy spot he'd worn down over time like a sand crab. A perfect mold of his body with the incline making a natural prop for his back. He let the warmth drip into his pores, saturating his skin like oil.

No soldiers hovered. Everything was fine, he decided. Just possibly, he was the boy's last-minute reprieve. Unorthodox, but why not? He watched a rowboat glide across the lake. A female guardian paddled forward while another guardian lounged at the back. Two humans sat in the middle, dragging their fingers in the water. The sun burned brighter in the center of the lake and both guardians were already a deep copper. After a few minutes, the two angels stood up in the boat to switch places, laughing as they balanced in the wobbly dinghy. They held onto each other's arms to steady themselves before crossing. Ohj watched intently, waiting to see if they capsized the boat, humans and all.

Red dropped down beside him, making him jump. "What's this about a rush court session?"

Hearing a splash, Ohj looked back to the lake and caught the tail of a fish. Still upright, the boat paddled onward, then in a lazy circle. A duck followed behind. "I don't know about any rushes."

"It's your case. Scheduled at the last minute. You're in my court today, so you must know something."

Ohj remained calm. "Is it the murdering pedophile, Wayne Matheson?"

"That's the name. A pedophile—great. I usually get more of break between your cases. Hope you're not starting a trend." He tossed a red bundle onto Ohj's lap. "I almost forgot."

Ohj caught it before it slid to the ground and held up the t-shirt with the words in white: No Appeals, No Last Meals. His longtime motto didn't seem half as clever as it used to.

"I know it's not your color; which is exactly why I picked it." Red pulled out some spongy bread from his pocket and threw it to a goose. The bread went ignored.

Ohj rolled the shirt up and jammed it behind him to use as a pillow. "Thanks."

"We missed you at Ronald's party."

"Can't wait for the pictures."

"You shouldn't make light about it. That was incredible. How often does a person make such restitution that their accounts aren't even read? Do you know how many times that's happened in my presence?" Red leaned forward, breaking Ohj's line of vision. "Seriously, how many?"

Ohj just wanted the moment to pass. "Six?"

"Hardly ever." Red leaned back again. "People turn down every opportunity to save themselves. No matter how many chances they get. When finally, *finally,* one person out of a million stinkin' cases comes along who gets it, it's huge. And Ronald's case will live on as one of those: a bottom-of-the-ninth thrill. You're just so used to winning every one of your cases, this threw you off. You aren't used to being challenged. Usually no one dares."

"You got it wrong. No one challenges me because I'm always right. That said, this has nothing to do with my pride. Don't make it a pride-issue." Ohj stared at the water as the bread Red threw bobbed near two downy swans. "So, what happened to that guardian dragged away in chains?"

"Now that's a tragedy. You understand I'm not at liberty to discuss the details, but he was found guilty. Obvious he was, by the way he fought the soldiers. Can you imagine fighting with soldiers?"

Ohj weighed his words. "Crazy."

"To say the least. What a scene. Right at the court entrance, no less."

"What will happen to him?"

"That's still undecided." Red offered a piece of the same bread to a rabbit who hopped in close. A black panther zeroed in on the cottontail, its unblinking, yellow eyes glowing between the branches of a nearby bush.

So far, they were down one angel and up a torturer. Ohj sighed. "We made a bad trade yesterday."

Red got up. "Stop moping and cheer up, because what happened at Ronald's trial was a fluke. Wear your new shirt with all the confidence that it won't happen again to you." He pulled out the last bit of bread from his pocket and threw it into the water. "Don't be late. I like to get your cases over with first."

"I'll be there."

The words sounded a gong in Ohj's head: *what happened was a fluke..., won't happen again....* Everything that he'd been through recently was nothing more than an anomaly. The universe continued to exist, still redeeming or not redeeming, despite his miniscule event. That the one guardian would be punished for who knows what offense, now worried him, but he had his own problems—like Wayne's trial.

Ohj moved fast. He'd never written down Wayne's last account. There would be no books waiting in court.

Red had already climbed half the steps to the courthouse when Ohj rushed behind to finish his work. As he moved, he mentally put himself back at Wayne's kitchen. Once he got to his room, he was ready. He threw the red t-shirt over the back of his chair and let the details fly onto the paper: foil, dead terrier, vinyl sheeting. The window began warming up. Deliberately keeping his back to it, Ohj reported on Wayne's utility scissors, and what terrible things he'd attempted to do with them.

After that, the wording got tricky. He stopped and straightened his shoulders. Up until Wayne slid on the dog entrails, the account was routine. Now he had to get creative: lie.

Why, or even how, Wayne died had no bearing on the crime, he told himself. Wayne was just as guilty and still deserved the harshest sentence possible. Ohj rubbed his temples, trying to think. Behind him, the window waited, fully warmed. He wished it had an on/off switch, or at least a dimmer.

He couldn't write the last words fast enough: *Wayne slipped and died.* The words were ridiculously vague, and he dreaded having to read them out loud before the court. The window kept up an incessant purring. Ohj dropped the pen and slammed shut the book. While he gathered up Wayne's other three hefty books, the purring had turned into an annoying whir.

The second he stood in front of the window, it crackled into full focus. The view was of a hotel room.

Ohj grimly scoped the room, making his mental notes. Typical décor: modern art bolted to beige walls, and carpet dark enough to camouflage sperm, urine or blood. A 32-inch TV blasted porn at a level loud enough to mask any personal noise, but not so loud that the family next door would call the front desk.

The bedspread was thrown on the floor, possibly so that the guest wouldn't touch what the blanket had absorbed over the last three months. He noted a Rolex and a thick wallet on the dresser next to the TV. At the same time, he took note of Tex, short for Frank, handcuffed to the bed by leopard print, padded handcuffs. Naked, except for a bolo string tie with a silver bull slide. Tex was 67 years old and should have known better than to let a complete stranger cuff him to a bed. A lifetime of wealth granted him invincibility. Now he was fearless enough to also wear a leather tie around his neck while his hands were shackled.

He'd taken two Viagra, which had already given him a solid erection. Now, he patiently watched porn, waiting for the date he hired to finish changing.

Carla, blonde curls bouncing, burst out of the bathroom in a thong and mismatched black bra. A red bandanna was tied around her neck in a saucy knot. "I see you're ready for me."

Chapter Three

Carla's breasts were large and very lopsided, a full cup-size difference between them. So self-conscious about her implants, she could hardly stand to take her shirt off even when alone. One breast drooped, its nipple pointing right at where her tummy tuck should be.

That was what brought her to Ohj's window—to earn the money for her breasts and stomach. She had no reservations earning it the old-fashioned way. But Carla wasn't a prostitute as Tex thought. She was a con artist. And he happened to be her target, with his Rolex, expensive suit, and arrogant horniness

The handcuffs had come with him; she'd planned to use duct tape. Since Ohj had never met her before, he guessed her crimes were going to escalate from here on.

Carla decided to entertain herself before robbing Tex. His overnight bag sat on the floor, filled with sticky toys, which she found repulsive for a man the age of her grandfather. She pulled the bag onto the sheets and picked through the bits and pieces, finally deciding on a bottle of flavored, warming gel.

Ohj tried to focus on the scene and not think about court, which he probably held up. He tried not to imagine that Red and Wayne's guardian were comparing notes and details of the trial.

"Oooh, 'hot, nubilla cream,'" Carla read off the label. She popped open the spigot and started squirting the lubricant on Tex, starting at his pole of an erection. After looping the gel around and around, making him quiver, she squirted a line all the way up his hairy chest.

"That stuff tastes real good." Tex' upper dentures wobbled from his wide grin. "Why don't you try some?"

Carla grabbed her throat. "Nubilla vanilla makes me puke." She ran the bottle round and round in an oval on his stomach, squeezing the container empty.

Tex started squirming. "Honey, that's industrial strength, and it's startin' to burn. Do ol' Tex a favor and lick it off."

"Oh, hell no. Don't want that crap in my mouth. And I'm not talking about the goop." She went back to the bag and pulled out nipple clamps. She snapped them both on Tex, also catching a few gray hairs.

"Uh, ok there — but those are really for you," Tex said. "Hey, why don't you try them on instead? Then come on up and ride Tex, like 'Hi ho, Silver, away.'"

"I don't know what the hell you're talking about." Carla reached back in and pulled out an enormous, purple dildo, holding it between a finger and her thumb. "Good lord. Hoping to molest an elephant? Someone should've warned the zoo you're in town." She tossed the nubby toy back.

With a shrug, she dropped the bag on the floor and went for her purse. Her blonde wig drooped forward, partially concealing her blue contacts. She pushed the hair back in place and took out a cigarette.

"Honey, this here's a no-smokin' room," Tex said.

Carla lit the cigarette with her Ed Hardy lighter and grabbed his wallet from the dresser. She exhaled smoke as she walked back to the bed, waving the wallet in front of her. "I wanna play a new game."

"Now, you're gonna get in trouble with that. Go and put that back where it belongs and come and ride your horsey."

She pulled out his debit card and a wad of cash; more than she'd hoped for, judging how her eyes widened at the $100 bill at the top. "This is the new game: you're gonna give me your PIN number, and then I'm gonna ride my horsey down the street to the ATM."

Tex yanked hard on the cuffs. "Hey, there. I'm payin' you enough as it is."

"You didn't let me finish the rules." She took the bandanna off her neck and started wadding it up. "You give me the right PIN, I'll let you live long enough for the maid to find you in the morning."

"Shit!" Tex turned red. "I have a family." He jerked hard on the bed again, until it banged against the wall.

"...if the PIN is wrong," she continued, as she crossed the room for her purse, "I kill you slowly until you give me the right one." She pulled out the roll of duct tape and came back to the bed. Letting the cigarette dangle between her lips, she tore off a five-inch strip of tape and bent over to look Tex in the eyes.

"Either way, I still get the mon-...." The cigarette dropped out. It bounced off his chest, rolled down his side, and landed on the bed next to him. A couple hot ashes flew up, burning the pink flesh over his ribs.

"Hey, now!" As he tried to pull away, the cigarette rolled towards him even faster, getting jammed between him and the mattress. "4349! 4349!"

"Dang it." She thrust her hand underneath him coming back out with the cigarette. She stuck the filter between her lips and took a puff. "That was fast. But wise decision on your part." After shoving the balled-up bandana inside his mouth, she slapped the duct tape over it.

"Shit—what was that number again? 3439?"

Tex shook his head.

"3449? I know it ended in nine. 4349?"

Tex nodded frantically. Carla wrote the number on her palm with the hotel pen. "OK, I'll be right back." She got dressed in her pretend, high-class hooker clothes, and left Tex and Ohj to their own devices.

Ohj sighed, wishing he hadn't opened the window. He should have just let it buzz all day while he got his business done in court. This could take hours. He knew Tex was going to die, correct PIN number or not. Carla wouldn't let him live long enough to describe her to the police. Now he was stuck babysitting while Carla ran errands.

Ohj stood at his window and watched Tex and his erection watch porn. Incredibly, Tex wasn't afraid for his life. All he worried about was how he was going to keep this incident from his wife and kids. But he wasn't even overly worried about that, since this was California, and his family lived in Texas. The PIN number was right, so Tex figured that once Carla robbed him of all the money the machine would spit out, a couple hundred, she would be on her way. Probably not even come back. As far as Tex was concerned, he only had to wait for the maid to make her embarrassing discovery, sometime before noon. Then he would get on his way to the airport, right after a long, hot shower.

Ohj wasn't as optimistic. Carla was coming back; she'd left the Rolex on the dresser. Plus, she still had to kill Tex.

Grunting and moaning filled the room as a uniformed delivery guy on TV showed up to deliver his package to two nurses.

Ohj's mind wandered back to court. Not a good idea to keep Red and Wayne's guardian waiting. He'd wanted to be there to hit them hard with the terrible details; not give them time to ask questions and look for coincidences. If they had time to think things through, the situation could get complicated. He rolled his eyes, growing as frustrated as Tex.

Now wearing a trench coat and hat, Carla finally unlocked the door. Ohj sank a bit from relief.

"You were right—the number's good. That was sure smart because I planned on hurting you pretty bad. No idle threat there." She went to climb up but, repulsed by the vanilla gel and his nakedness, stopped to yank the blanket and sheets up over him.

Tex' eyes widened when she straddled him. He started thrashing as she took his Bolo tie in both her hands. After he almost bucked her off, she moved up higher on his chest. She twisted the little leather strips around her hand, looping them tight enough to cut into his skin. Then she twisted once more, tighter, and held, until he quit rearing.

"Hi ho silver away," she said, as his eyes bugged.

She turned off the TV, grabbed the Rolex and left.

Ohj's window closed.

Before running out, Ohj remembered just in time to cleanse. He dipped in his hands, and splashed water on his face and body before changing.

He didn't stop moving until he hit his mark in front of Red's podium in the courtroom. No one seemed to care he was late. He drummed his fingers on the books as he waited for them to bring in Wayne, all the while scanning the crowd for special guests.

Wayne was dragged in after Red called his name. When Red asked for the witness, Ohj fought the urge to look behind him. This time he was the only one in front.

"I have it on authority that this will be a violent case," Red warned the room. "If anyone wishes to leave, now would be a good time."

Six guardians stood up. As they walked past Ohj, one touched him sadly. "I'm sorry," the guardian mouthed.

"For what?" Ohj quickly mouthed back.

After the court settled, Ohj read his accounts: all four of them. Three little boys before Garrett died while tied to Wayne's kitchen table. He relived the horrible crimes along with the spectators, sparing no one. Guardians cried openly. More had to leave the room, disrupting Ohj's reading. Red called a halt to the testimony twice to compose the courtroom.

During the testimony, Wayne stayed in a shaking heap at the platform. "please help me, please help me..., I'm sorry..., I'm sorry...." He mumbled at the floor as his trial went on around him.

When the testimony came to its abrupt end, Red showed not suspicion over Ohj, but relief that it was over. A guilty sentence rang out and the room filled with bright light. The sentence was good.

No one cheered as the guards hauled Wayne off to face an eternity of torment. Neither were tears spilled on his behalf. Too frightened to walk, Wayne slid past Ohj, dragged towards a long passageway. The walkway got darker the further out it went from Ohj's view. It eventually went black: shadows suffocating every bit of residual sunshine. Ohj had never walked down that passage, never cared to discover where it led.

But this time his eyes lingered. Even after Wayne was hauled out of view, Ohj tried to see into the dark recess.

After a few moments, he shook off his stupor and dropped his gaze. Around his shoes the floor sparkled silver. Reading Garrett's ordeal had taken its toll. He scattered the sparkles with his foot. From a corner of his eyes he gauged if anyone was close enough to notice his flaked skin on the ground. The courtroom was too busy preparing for the next case.

He kicked the last bits away and walked out, feeling like he had just escaped a noose.

A little breathless, he wandered across the grass and sat down on the first bench in his path. Before he could rethink his choice of a seat, a guardian dropped down next to him: the same bold guardian who had crashed his tub in the soaking room. Wordlessly, Ohj looked around at the empty benches surrounding them, counting at least seven to choose from. While the guardian looked ahead at the water, Ohj wasn't as polite and stared right at him. Plain jeans and t-shirt, rough brown shoes with thin laces, the guardian dressed casually. No jewelry or markings, and his head was bare, except for the short, white-blonde ringlets.

He finally turned to Ohj. "I couldn't resist taking this seat. I hope you don't mind."

"You couldn't resist?" Ohj asked. "What's it about that spot? I'd like to know, so I can grab it first next time."

The guardian's smile set off his sapphire-blue eyes, and one dimple surfaced near his mouth. His soft, light blue shirt favored the gold shine of his skin. He raised one shoulder in a half shrug. "I notice that you get left alone. Either you're crazy important or everyone's afraid of you. I figure if I sit with you, I'll get left alone too. If I take any one of those other seats...." He gestured at a bench where a guardian was easing down between two others and a sleeping badger. "...The odds are, someone will plop down next to me."

Even as he talked, the empty benches filled up. Animated chatter floated all the way over to Ohj, threatening him with a bad mood. The blonde was right. There wasn't one other bench Ohj would dare sit on.

"I actually saw someone twisting balloons together," the blonde continued. "Those long skinny birthday party balloons. What's the deal, anyway?"

Ohj leaned back. "Everyone's just very happy. And kids love balloons."

"I don't care. I'm not wearing an inflated crown—or walk a poodle on a stick." The guardian scooted to the edge of the seat and crossed his legs out in front of him. "I'm Vincent, by the way." Stretching his hand out toward Ohj, he kept it extended until Ohj finally grabbed on to shake.

"A guardian?" Doubt turned Ohj's statement into a question. Vincent had the size of a guardian: not as muscle-bound as a witness. He also had the required gentle face: adequately pleasing to soothe a child with a scraped knee or lure his charge out of the path of an oncoming car. Only, the attitude was different.

"I am, but I still want to sit without anyone bothering me." Vincent waved off an approaching eagle, talons extended to use the back of their bench as a perch. "I'm here waiting for my next assignment. As peaceful as this place is, I don't seem to get any peace." He finally returned Ohj's hard stare. Ohj didn't flinch.

With his blonde hair and dolly face, Vincent kind of reminded him of Carla, the con artist from the hotel.

"You don't smoke, do you? Cuz you look like you do."

Vincent dropped the stare and turned back to the sun. "And get a bucket of confetti thrown on me?"

Ohj was starting to like him. He tried to visualize the park through the eyes of a newcomer: it was a little circus-like. One of the first stopping places for souls, the country spot couldn't be more tolerant, giving guardians and people permission to exist how they wanted. Sometimes beings took advantage. But as far as Ohj could tell, the only judge of bad taste here seemed to be him. Excitement filled the air as if everyone knew something wonderful was about to happen. Spectacular views. Wild animals milling around as if tame. Every day as glorious as the last. Perfect freedom. What's not to be excited about?

He and all the other witnesses answered that question every time they testified in court. They burst all the bubbles, wiped off all the smiles.

"So, do people leave you alone cuz you hurt them?" Vincent asked him.

"How, and why, would I hurt anyone?"

Vincent eyed him from behind a fallen curl. "Well, you look like you want to. Also, you have to be the shiniest creature I've ever seen: it physically hurts me to look at you."

"Whatever it takes."

With Vincent protecting the other side of the bench, Ohj started to get down to the business of recharging. If Vincent would quit talking now, the temporary arrangement might work. Before Ohj had the chance to settle in, he caught sight of someone just beyond Vincent's curls. In his formal attire and commanding presence, the High Witness was impossible to miss. Especially since he headed for Ohj's bench.

This was the first time he'd seen him here in the park. All the High Witnesses stayed in the City with the important action. Nothing happened here that created much interest. What were the odds this one witness would be back so soon? Not to apologize, he was sure. A guardian had glommed onto him. The High Witness stopped to chat, as graciously as if signing an autograph.

Ohj wasn't a fan. He turned back to the lake. Every so often he checked the High Witness' actions with a flick of his eyes. The guardian kept the conversation going, gesturing with his hands as he told some story. When he got free of the chatty guardian, the High Witness headed towards the bench. Ohj braced himself. He didn't want to talk or debate their last trial. Definitely didn't want to find out that the being just landed a new job alongside him in Red's court.

Instead of coming straight to Ohj, the High Witness missed the bench by several feet.

"A friend of yours?" Vincent asked.

"We used to fight battles together. A long time ago."

Ohj nodded in acknowledgement first. The Witness lifted a hand. Neither smiled. If Ohj were a friendly sort, he would wave him over. Instead, he settled for the awkward long-distance greeting.

"He's boring a hole between my eyes," Vincent complained. "Was he always so stalker-like?"

"Don't know." Ohj continued to watch the High Witness. "We weren't buddies." They just did as much damage as fast as they could. Killed legions. If he were completely honest, he'd admit that he loved every minute. "We got the job done, like machines."

"Now you're just two old retired guys, hanging out in the park together. That's sweet." Vincent stretched his arms over his head and yawned. "Don't invite him over. He gives me the creeps."

"No problem."

The crowd went quiet. Bustling stopped as everyone looked upwards at hundreds of new clouds in the once-clear sky. The clouds, little wispy singular puffs, floated closer together until they connected with a soft kiss. One big cloud began to grow overhead. All remaining little puffs drifted across the sky, aiming for that mass. Everyone stared up, except Ohj and Vincent, until they found themselves sitting in the shade.

"That's great," Ohj moaned, looking down at his hungry skin. It seemed to instantly shrivel. "No reason for me to stay."

"Hopefully, I'll be gone soon too...." Vincent started, as Ohj walked off.

As he left the grass, Ohj searched the area for the High Witness. The being wasn't in view: hopefully the last time he visited for a long while.

He'd proved that he was officially back to his old self with Carla and Tex at the hotel—didn't even twitch as Carla strangled the man in cold blood. The act didn't faze him a bit. That alone showed that he should still be working his room.

The window hummed invitingly. He went up to it like an old friend.

It opened to a wooden pier jutting over a lake. Ohj took in the scene: cold, overcast night with a biting wind and a whiff of ozone. Jaime sat in the passenger seat of a white mustang. Her husband, Edward, slumped over the wheel, asleep due to a sleeping pill flavored margarita. With Edward unconscious, the car seemed destined to roll off the pier and sink into the water below. The only thing stopping the car from diving in was Jaime's foot, stretched over the center console to push down on the brake. The passenger's window was down: while the driver's window remained up. If the electrical system gave out, the doors would remain hopelessly locked.

Ohj stayed relaxed, knowing the woman struggled with her decision. Jaime felt trapped in a bad marriage, but oddly, she felt more trapped by the course she'd set into motion this night. The wind rushed in through her open window, chilling her despite her thick sweater. To get her foot off the brake, she reminded herself of the waiting warm bath and hot pot of coffee. She also buoyed herself by thinking of a planned, non-refundable cruise paid by her friend from work. At that moment that same co-worker warmed the bath for her.

A surge of decisiveness got her foot over to the accelerator. The Mustang lurched forward and flew off the pier. When the car began to drop, she squeezed her eyes shut. The impact jolted her hard and she bit her tongue. Water rushed in through her window, causing the car to tip. Her side was going down first. She screamed in panic and grabbed onto the handle to try to open the door. Fear sent her into shock.

She'd waited too long for an easy exit and had to fight against the current of water gushing inside. Breathing through the pain of the freezing cold, she pushed her head out through the open window.

The rushing water revived Edward. It took him a few seconds to realize that his night terror was real. "Jaime," he cried, grabbing onto her ankle.

She kicked him off and pushed the rest of her body out of the sinking car.

"Jaime. Jaime, wait...." He fumbled with his seatbelt.

Jaime swam the ten yards to the shore and climbed onto the bank. The backpack she'd left behind remained safe on the pier. She moved fast, shivering as she stripped off her wet clothes, balling them into a plastic grocery bag.

After throwing the backpack over her shoulder, she sprinted away in dry sweats.

The warning lights on the dashboard colored Edward's freezing tomb an eerie red. Finally, he got the seatbelt unlatched, but now had to get to the open passenger window. Instead of making that quick exit, he pounded on his own window and tried to push open his door, wasting precious seconds. The car finished filling up, while he still pushed helplessly.

Ohj shook his head, keeping his attention on the submerged car. A guardian went into the water. They both waited for irreversible brain damage, Edward's last reflexive gasp, and finally death.

Ohj opened a new book, the first on Jaime, and wondered if this one would even reach court. The odds were in her favor that during her next thirty years, she would fall to her knees, beg forgiveness, and swear very earnestly that she would never kill again. And she would probably mean it.

Alarmed by his lingering negative thoughts about the human, he set the pen down.

After a couple moments, he pulled his hair back and tucked the loose black strands behind his ears. Then he picked up the pen again to give Jaime the unbiased account she deserved. The window began to light up. He rubbed his eyes and kept writing.

Though he knew about her affair, he didn't witness it, so that detail wouldn't make it into his account. His account began with the car idling on the pier and ended with Edward's final breaths. The dry clothes waiting for her to change into, and the fact she kicked Edward away when he reached for help: those details were also written down. And the detail that she didn't cave at the end and offer a hand to pull him up for air, so they could laugh about the incident over a bottle of wine.

Whirring buzzed his ears. With a kick of his foot, the chair swiveled until he faced the window. When he stood up, instead of walking to the scene, he headed out the hallway.

He leaned against the outside of his room, running his hands through his hair. He pushed the strands back, too short for a ponytail, only to have them fall forward again. He set off down the corridor to let the colors calm any lingering resentment. Back and forth; cool, blue walls, cool, blue thoughts.

Cool, blue walls, cool, blue thoughts.

By the time he reached his window, he was in control. And confident.

The orange grove was filled with rows of thick-rooted trees, planted decades before. Their clean lines seemed to run forever. The dirt between the trees was swept of weeds and leaves, and the orange blossoms shrouded the grove in a blizzard of perfume. Ohj loved that scent and wished he could savor it for just a moment.

A breeze picked up a few loose blossoms and dropped them delicately onto an eight-year-old girl, sitting in the dirt. Her backpack, with her leftover lunch and homework, leaned up against a tree. A large rock, a few inches away, waited to crush her skull.

A man bustled near the girl: Lloyd, another regular of Ohj's. Seventeen girls suffered at this man's hands. He buried most but dumped some when he was in a hurry. He debated his options now, as she hugged the doll he'd given to quiet her.

It was just a rag doll he'd picked up at a dollar store, but it felt soft, and its string hair was her favorite color—lime green. She watched him sadly, sensing something bad was about to happen, as he dug through his rucksack.

Ohj heard the migrant workers first. Two of them had stayed behind to work the off-season for some extra cash. Lloyd chose the orange grove because it wasn't orange-picking season. He figured that by the time the season started, the mound of dirt that covered the little girl would be nicely weathered— the perfect gravesite. He hadn't planned on workers being in the grove, of all days.

Four rows over, the workers looked around for any weeds or debris.

Lloyd jumped on the girl and held his hand over her mouth. He didn't have to hush her; she was too scared to yell. Still, he covered her mouth; hard enough for his fingers to cast an impression on her cheeks. She continued to hold the doll, now pressed between them.

The migrant workers stayed in their row, talking about a local, cheap dentist. Lloyd monitored them through the tree trunks. He glanced at her backpack. The workers only had to turn their heads a little more to the left and they would see the bright pink pack. If they then followed it, looking a little further, they would see him. He held his breath and cursed himself for not leaving the pack with the shovel in the car.

Luckily for Lloyd, the workers didn't look beyond the one dirt path they patrolled. They kept walking ahead, finally wandering out of sight. Hearing their truck engine fire up, he let go of the girl and rolled onto his back. His big belly heaved with relief.

He smiled. "We're safe now." After breathing a minute, he sat up and leaned against a tree. He whistled softly as he reached into his pocket.

At sixty-two, Lloyd could continue to live a long, active life. How many more events like this one would Ohj have to witness for him?

The girl twisted some strings of yarn doll hair around one finger. She pulled the little doll to her mouth and whispered faintly, "Help. I'm scared."

Ohj knew the quiet prayer wasn't meant for him. Even so, he walked through his window and stepped onto the dirt.

Chapter Four

The journey took a fraction of a second, and wasn't difficult, like pushing past surface tension. But the pressure of the physical world enveloped him instantly, pressing hard on every inch of his body. And the cold; like he dove into ice water. Without the shield of the window, human pain of every kind was packed into one bullet. Normally the window sheltered him from the onslaught of pain. Not just physical pain and anguish as people faced death, but also trauma from previous abuse and life in general. This new bullet wound created an imprint on his brain, as clear as his own memories.

The little girl's terror ripped at his heart. Her fear and confusion assaulted him so forcefully he might as well have been the cause. Other than her current distress, the girl had a happy past, nothing traumatic for Ohj to sense.

Lloyd was another story.

If Ohj had stayed behind the window he would have been protected from Lloyd. Even though Ohj was present during all of Lloyd's assaults, saw his heart and knew his motives, he'd never *experienced* it. But breathing the same air as this monster was like turning up the power to maximum. Thirty-five years of depravity, rape, and murder hit Ohj in the head and gut.

Ohj also inhaled the air of evil, ancient creatures. With his perverse history, Lloyd managed to attract a large group. They were drawn to the human's indecent aura, as much as Ohj was repelled by it.

Demons always scattered when Ohj appeared to witness. They had very good reasons to fear him; he'd butchered enough of them over the ages. Cowardly, they rarely allowed him a glimpse. Now, even though he hadn't caught the blur of the retreating fiends, it was obvious by the rotten stench they'd been there. Because of the size of the noxious cloud, Ohj guessed they were too numerous to count.

Ohj moved to stand in front of the girl, shielding her from the molester's energy. Mindlessly, Lloyd busied himself, setting down paper towels, so he wouldn't dirty his belongings.

If the girl sensed that something protected her, she didn't let on. With Ohj blocking his view, Lloyd wouldn't notice right away if she jumped up. She only needed a running start; Lloyd didn't have the stamina to catch up with an eight-year-old. It would take several seconds just for him to pull all his excess weight to his feet. But unaware of her opportunity, the girl didn't move.

The closeness to the pedophile sickened Ohj. As Lloyd dwelled on past pleasures, he took Ohj on the journey with him, soaking Ohj's brain with cruelty and pain. With one finger, Ohj tapped the pedophile once on the top of his skull. Lloyd dropped his plastic jar in the dirt and slid over onto his side. The awful memories stopped.

The girl was safe for now.

Ohj went back to his room. Physical relief flooded over him, like sliding back into a warm pool. He took a deep breath to clear the worldly pressure from his lungs then looked back at the scene.

The girl remained in the dirt, eyes squeezed shut, the doll pushed against her forehead with both hands. Lloyd hadn't moved either, propped up by his belly.

"Run," Ohj urged her softly. "Get up now and run."

The little girl peeked through the green yarn. Ohj tensed, and got ready to walk back in.

Keeping her eyes on her attacker, the little girl slowly got up. First on her knees, then up, one foot at a time. On his side, watery eyes open just a fraction, the pedophile didn't try to stop her. The girl looked down on him as she began to side step. Ohj started to go in to spur her on when her guardian arrived. A tall male with aquamarine eyes and hair tumbling to his shoulders, the guardian gently turned her away from the man on the ground. He then aimed her by her shoulders out of the grove of trees.

Ohj exhaled. "You're ok, get up," he told the pedophile. "I didn't hit you that hard. You're fine. Get up."

The pedophile didn't move. The window went dark.

"Crap."

He hung his head and went to his desk to write up what was now going to be Lloyd's last account. The words spilled easily at first: the off-season orange grove/convenient burial place, the preoccupied migrant workers who looked away at the last minute, the doll, the backpack. The words came to a stop at the part after Lloyd laid out the paper towels. Again — how was he going to explain this death? A coconut dropped out of the sky?

He wiped off his upper lip and wrote the words quickly: collapsed, fell into unconsciousness, died.

In his antechamber, he stripped off his clothes, peeling them inside out, so they wouldn't touch his skin. The smell of putrid, rotting flesh rose off the fabric. He drenched a wash cloth and scoured his face, even scrubbing at the insides of his nostrils. He took a mouthful of the water, and gargled it at the back of his throat, before spitting it out on the floor. He raked the cloth across his arms and legs. Then again, dipping the cloth into the water over and over, leaving the bowl empty, and wishing there was a little more for one more rinse.

A towel in each hand, he scraped more than dried, shaking the towels off then going at it again. A heap of stinking clothes and soaked towels lay on the floor. Ignoring the conspicuous shine of skin that intertwined the wet mound, he folded the last towel and placed it on top. A fresh silver handprint, where he pushed the stack down, decorated the pile like a Christmas bow.

Now he needed direct, preferably blistering, sun.

He wondered if he appeared different. He felt different—naked. Two witnesses walked directly in his path, coming at him a few yards apart from each other. From the corner of his eye, he checked for the slightest reaction. The first, a head-shaved, battle scared female, didn't as much as glance at him as she passed. The second kept his focus on the ground.

He glided down the grass, winding around the other visitors, until he reached his little burrow in the hill.

No one bothered to look his way. All eyes were on an enormous moose that walked in the lake. The moose followed the water's edge, taking large loping steps that barely made a splash. Antlers spanned as wide as the animal stood tall, and its fur was so thick the water dripped off in rivulets. Guardians cooed at the beautiful animal, trying to get it to come close enough for several children to pet. It stopped walking to dip its nose in the clear water. To the delight of the young crowd, it dunked its antlers in and lifted its head back out with a shake. Ignoring the group onshore, the moose started to plod along again.

Ohj grimaced at the guardian's catcalls, inches from his head. The squeals and shouts got louder when swans rushed in, swimming towards the moose as if in a race. The moose ambled just off the shoreline, pulling the little crowd of guardians and children along with it, until they blocked Ohj's view of the water. After a minute, the birds gave up and paddled back in a white parade. The guardians led the kids off to another place of interest.

Red emerged from the throng, waving at Ohj as he headed towards him. Ohj looked away, pretending not to see him. He had a new unplanned trial: another dead killer, which again begged the question; why did the murderer die, and the victim live? Having to avoid this explanation in court was bad enough. But here came Red for a personal interrogation.

Ohj got up to make a run for it.

"Not one, but two today, Ohj?" Red called out to him.

Ohj searched his memory. "Two? I should only have one: a child killer."

Ohj scrambled for who the second case belonged to. "Refresh me on the cases: Lloyd the pedophile, and...?"

"A man—had a history of driving while intoxicated—once killed a family of four.... I'd love to tell you more, but the books aren't there."

"Drunk driver? Drunk driver...?" Ohj raised his hands in defeat.

"Name is, Paul. Ring any bells?"

Ohj's head dropped forward. Paul, the drunk driver. That seemed like eons ago. "I forgot about Paul. I'll go get his reports."

"Real quick." Red grabbed his arm. "Remember that guardian detained in front of the courthouse?" He stopped to gaze up at the sky. It turned a deep blue just above them, just dark enough to highlight new faintly pink waves of clouds. Orange and salmon hues began to shine around the edges as flashes of light lit the rollers from behind. "Truly amazing," Red whispered.

Ohj felt a nervous flutter in his stomach. Of course, he remembered the angel. Instead of looking up at the display, he waited for Red to continue. He gave him a few extra seconds before interrupting the sight. "So, what happened to him—the guardian?"

Red kept his neck craned upward. "He's in charge of keeping the City Park beautiful now."

If Ohj wasn't so tense, he would've laughed out loud. "No kidding? The guardian's what—a park ranger?"

A guardian who didn't have to follow some human around anymore? That wasn't a punishment: it was a promotion, though Ohj wouldn't say it out loud. "He deserved what he got. But I'm sure the park will never look better," he said without a smile.

Leaving Red to enjoy the sky, he walked away slowly, trying to remember Paul, the drunk driver.

Did he kill him?

A mob flowed out, blocking the path on either side. A guardian had started a mock wrestling match with a man on the lawn. The guardian was bigger and stronger than the human, even though the pro wrestler brought his youth and best shape into the afterlife with him. After the guardian tossed the wrestler to the grass repeatedly, the crowd started complaining about the unfair odds. To appease them, the guardian tied his arm to his side with a scarf. He created a show of how helpless he now was, with just the one arm to throw the man to the ground with.

Ohj sighed as he tried to push past the group. The crowd cheered the human on, which started his guardian laughing. The growling human attempted to toss the guardian down, making the guardian laugh so hard he fell to the ground useless. The wrestler took advantage and jumped on top of the angel, pinning him down. The man then popped up and flexed both arms, fists above his ears. "No one can beat *The Bouncer*. I dare anyone to try." He turned in a slow circle as he growled. "No one. You want to try?" he asked a smiling guardian.

The guardian held up his hands in instant defeat.

The wrestler pointed at a large witness. "You—yeah, I'm talking to *you*; the bald guy trying to sneak off." Easy to spot, the witness towered over everyone else, his biceps bigger than all of their heads. Like Ohj, the witness was making his way around the crowd. "Wanna be next?" the wrestler shouted.

The witness turned his bald head slightly to glance at the man but didn't stop walking. His leathers were embedded with bone fragments, and his shoes were as thick as truck tires, ready to roll over anyone who had the courage to get in front of them. The guardian closest to the man shook his head at him. Another put a finger to her lips.

Missing the cues, the man again shouted to the witness, "What? Are you coward? Afraid to match up against *The Bouncer*? Come on—let's go!" He clapped his hands together with long loud claps, easily heard over the shoulders of the guardians trying to shield him.

Ohj laughed when the entire mob hushed. Finally entertained, he stopped pushing bodies out of his way.

Ohj yelled at the witness himself. "Hey baldy, why you running away?" He squeezed in between a couple of angels, until he stood at the inner circle, then cupped his hands around his mouth. "Is the big, bald chicken afraid of losing even more feathers?"

The witness stopped and turned to face the human. The mob went solemn.

Ohj couldn't help himself. "Afraid you'll get that ginormous butt handed to you in a sling?"

The witness searched the crowd for the source of the mocking. The crowd parted quickly.

Trying not to smile, Ohj knew if the witness took the bait and came at him, he'd also start laughing too hard to fight back. The wrestler's guardian jumped up off the grass and pulled his person in line behind him. All angelic smiles evaporated.

So busy enjoying this response from the crowd, Ohj wasn't aware the witness was on the move until it was too late. The charging witness slammed him hard to the ground. The giant was as solid as concrete, landing on top of Ohj in one thick slab.

"Waitin' a long time for an offer this good," the witness breathed the words in Ohj's face. He eased off but left one knee buried in Ohj's stomach to hold him down. "Someone get me that sling!" He exhaled in snorts, while his kneecap inched in, digging into Ohj's diaphragm until he coughed.

Ohj pushed at the wall of muscle attached to the witness' thigh so that he could breathe, but the leg wouldn't budge. He then reached up to shove at the witness' chest. Again, the giant wouldn't be moved. It was like trying to move a skyscraper. Almost curious at his lack of strength, Ohj balled up his fist and threw a good punch. The hit didn't bounce off; more slid down, like a squeegee wiping off imaginary sweat.

The thought dawned on Ohj's that he wasn't himself physically. If he'd been aware of his new state, he would never have challenged a brute who used bones as a fashion statement. This made him wonder about his mental state: how could he have been so stupid?

A female witness broke through the crowd. Half dozen braids dissected her hair and her jeans were tucked into black motorcycle boots that appeared to have been strapped to her legs since the beginning of time. Fluid tattoos covered her arms: motion pictures of her conquests. She regarded the writhing men with disgust.

"I get the winner," she warned. Not one guardian argued.

The crowd remained quiet. The guardians started stepping back from the skirmish, which got uglier when the witness started slamming Ohj's head into the ground. He pressed his forearm down against Ohj's throat, then leaned in, again choking off Ohj's air supply. With his free fist, he started pounding Ohj's face. One blow closed both Ohj's eyes so that he couldn't see the one that slammed into his nose.

Ohj managed to pry off the arm long enough to rear up and head-butt the fierce witness. When the giant jerked back, Ohj tried to throw him off. He'd intended to fling him backwards several feet but had only enough oomph to push him up and over. Ohj followed the move all the way through, and rolled on top, gaining the upper hand over the behemoth. He waited for the cheers of the crowd, now that he, the underdog, finally got a leg up.

The crowd only saw the small rabbit that the two fighting witnesses had smashed in the initial tackle.

"Noooo," the guardians screamed simultaneously. The racket was so thunderous, that the giant let go of Ohj's neck. The two regarded the little flattened mass of fur lying next to them. Still straddling the witness, Ohj slid off.

The bunny's foot quivered. Three guardians almost knocked themselves out rushing in to grab the rabbit. As it rested in one guardian's arms, the rabbit started to show slight signs of life, moving an ear, taking a shallow breath. The guardian passed it on, hoping the next being could better restore the wounded creature. The bunny puffed up a bit, filling out its pelt. Soon it quivered and scratched to be put down.

The giant got up and dusted himself. By the time Ohj was back on his feet, the witness had disappeared. The female challenger rolled her eyes and went off in her own direction.

Ohj limped to work. Frowning, he massaged the bones in his hand back into place. He only got one hit in, and that one blow probably didn't leave even a slight bruise. If he didn't learn anything else this afternoon, he learned that he needed to bulk up.

He bumped into his cleaner again, still working on his room. The man stopped scooping up clothes to look at him. Ohj wasn't sure if the cleaner was more puzzled by the crazy mess of stained, wet towels and clothes, or the frequent interruptions. He'd only seen the man a few odd times before. Now they were in each other's laps.

"Sorry...what...," Ohj mumbled, walking past. He closed the door to the antechamber behind him, only to have it drift back open. The door had no catch on it. He'd never realized that it was a symbolic entrance, not a practical one. He grabbed a couple of finished books from beside his desk: Carla's one thin one, and a thicker book on Luis, a drug cartel underling. He dropped them on the ground and pushed them up against the door with his foot to keep it shut.

Then he sat down to read through Paul, the drunk driver's book. Reading the first page brought back more details, almost as if the details had gotten hazy over time, which was impossible. Did Paul pop a few open on the way, distracting him? Something else lay on the seat next to him—drugs? A gun?

What he was sure of, was that Paul was every bit alive the last time he saw him. He reread the end just to make sure. And no—he hadn't done the slightest thing to harm him in any way. If Paul just happened to hit a light pole, or have a massive heart attack later that week, no one could blame it on him.

He walked back to court, his face up, desperate for sustenance. Eyes shut, he concentrated on the orange glow that streamed through his eyelids. When he opened one eye a crack, he thought the freed torturer, Ronald Bass, came towards him. He blinked past the glare.

In the distance, Ronald and a companion made their way down the path. The pair headed in his direction, laughing. Ronald had a guitar thrown over his shoulder. The companion, a soft-faced woman with red curly hair, swung a picnic basket with both hands.

Ohj moved like a steam engine, gripping his books. Ronald's friend pointed to a zebra near the lake. At her direction, Ronald looked towards the water. Ohj gained speed, aiming right for Ronald's smile with drunk-driver Paul's books. With more muscle than he intended, Ohj hit Ronald face-on, sending him flying. His head bounced once, and the guitar splintered beneath him with a loud crash. A throng of angels ran over to help.

Ohj stood straight, ready for war, Ronald's blood pounding in his ears. He dropped his books on the ground to free up both hands. His fists were a lot more solid than the hardbacks, and he knew, weak or not, he could make Ronald fly farther the second time.

Ronald walked up to him laughing. The fractured guitar, still strapped to his back, dangled to the ground by the strings. "Wow. You're solid muscle. I'll be sure to give you more room next time I see you, friend."

Ronald strolled around him. As he continued to the lake, a guardian pulled a fresh guitar from out of nowhere. Ronald settled at the lake's edge and lifted the new instrument onto his lap. His companion pulled out red checkered napkins from the basket. The smell of fried chicken wafted along in the air.

Ohj picked up his books and headed for the court steps. As the doors closed behind him, he heard a voice from the park, "Hey, chocolate chip cookies."

When Red called the first case, Ohj looked at drunk-driver Paul through narrowed, blazing eyes.

Ohj sailed through his cases with clenched teeth, spitting out the ugly details of each crime: guilty and guilty.

They were all guiltier than sin.

"You can go to hell now." Ohj said to Lloyd, his last case. He slammed the book shut. "And I'm done."

Two guardians glanced over at him, while a nearby witness covered a smile with an account book. The guards stopped dragging Lloyd away and looked over to Red, in case Ohj's outburst earned the man a reprieve. Unsmiling, Red waved for them to continue. He then rapped on his platform to quiet the hum spreading through the room. Ohj turned away before Red felt the need to work the gavel again.

Outside, Ronald still played the guitar. A crowd had formed a circle around him. Ohj cringed. When the song ended, Ohj blew out his breath, until the music started up again.

At least at work no noise got in or out. Though he knew it was the last place he should go. He wasn't trustworthy there. But he couldn't be trusted with the crowd at the lake either. He was trapped. And he was neglecting his body. Every time he tried to refuel, something chased him away. Plus, it seemed to take longer to recharge. His cells were depleted, and his judgment clouded. He needed to just sit in quiet—and not think.

The window waited for him, already hot. As soon as he stepped close, it blinked into focus. A national bank appeared in front of him. One massive open room, with a line of customers snaking past a row of tellers. Four tellers, safely hidden behind partitions along with their cash, waved the customers over. To get their business done, each customer had to pass a table with offers of Visa cash cards, low mortgage rates, and bowls of hard candy.

Shadows skittered around the edges of the room. Creatures that normally hurried away, stuck around this time, loitering in the corners of the scene like juvenile delinquents. Black and slimy, the shadows slinked along the walls, shrinking together to camouflage themselves in a belt of assembled stink. Ohj had to force his attention away from them to study the humans in the scene.

A man at the back of the line wore a long hunting jacket and orange beanie. With deer season in full swing, no one paid attention. The unshaven man looked tired, as if up since daybreak to start the hunt. He pulled a Mini Uzi, Sub Machine Gun out from his hunting jacket and bumped the lady in line in front of him, knocking her wallet out of her hand. The lady puffed up and turned, coming face to face with the muzzle. She screamed. A wave of screams travelled up the line after each person woke from their personal daze and spotted the gun.

From the corner of his eye, Ohj saw a black mass begin to take shape. He refused to give it his attention.

The hunter pointed the Uzi at the security guard leaning against a wall. The guard put both hands up.

"Slide your gun over and get down on the ground," Troy said.

The guard cooperated. After unsnapping the holster, he took out his gun, slowly and deliberately. Then carefully slid it over, got down on his stomach, and stretched his hands above his head.

Gritting his teeth, Ohj flashed a quick look at the shadows slithering up on either side of the guard. They swarmed over his prone body until it appeared he was covered with a tarry blanket. They stayed so close to each other, he couldn't get a good head count.

The demons looked too comfortable as they weighed the man down, alluding to the fact they'd been together a long time.

A few feet away, the large black mass blinked at him with bloodshot eyes. He turned his attention back to Troy before he missed any more details.

Troy stood tall, over six feet, with barrels for arms and Tootsie Rolls for fingers. He kept his hair short, so only a little brown with scattered gray bristled out from under the beanie. Though far from old, just thirty-nine, his face was prematurely weathered from long hours in the sun, squinting through a rifle scope. At the same time, nightly trips to the local bar weathered his liver and internal organs. He put the security guard's gun under his waistband, then turned his Uzi on the row of tellers.

Like they were controlled by one mind, the entire row began shoving money into bags. Troy watched them through narrowed eyes. Cocking his head, he looked next at the row of customers. Under his gaze, they started emptying their purses and pockets. The customers tossed all their money and phones at Troy's feet, then began taking off their watches and jewelry. Troy let his gun sag as the cooperative group built a pile of loot on the tile in front of him.

Troy shouted out above the bustle, "Julia! Julia, where are you?" The customers in line didn't answer, but instead all got down, face first on the ground. Troy yelled at the top of his lungs: "Julia, get the fuck out here! You know what I'm here for."

The tellers stopped shuffling money and stared through their Plexiglas.

71

"I'm right here, Troy." A small woman buzzed herself out through a locked door. Thin and pale, she was no match for the beefy man with a gun. She wore gray polyester slacks, pink cardigan, and a small greasy demon that strung along behind like toilet paper stuck to her shoe.

The tellers now recognized Troy from last year's Christmas party—Julia's husband. He'd made a good impression at the time: didn't say much, or stare at anyone's breasts for too long. If he had talked at all, it was about some deer he'd bagged.

Ohj's eyes flickered on one slimy shadow as it stepped away from the rest of the quivering mass. It took a tentative step forward, as if testing him.

Julia walked towards Troy. She stopped a few yards away and waited for his next command. Her personal ogre hung around her ankles, peeking around to look at Ohj before slinking back.

The tellers should have been ducking but were too bewildered—and curious. The customers got up on their elbows to watch the scene unfold. Now they all just expected a bad fight. Maybe he caught her cheating. Or maybe she caught him cheating. Only the bank manager had the forethought to trigger the silent alarm. The five minutes the police needed to get there, and then the extra forty-five to organize back-up and negotiators, would be too long to help anybody inside.

The whispers from the demons droned like angry bees. Though Ohj strained to ignore it, an occasional word, "whore..., cunt...," rose above the human noise.

Troy hadn't caught Julia cheating, but was so convinced she had, she couldn't convince him otherwise. Every lurid detail had been reworked in his mind. His only regret was that her boyfriend didn't work at the bank. He figured, at least being a cop, the boyfriend would hear about her death soon enough.

In reality, Julia didn't know any policemen. She'd had one encounter where a cop had let her off the hook: not ticketing her for failing to slow down in a speed trap. The cop Troy pinned the affair on wasn't even the one who didn't fine her for speeding; he worked the next county over.

Ready to begin, Troy pointed the gun at the far end of the row of tellers. He wasn't targeting his rampage at Julia yet; he was first going after her friends. And he wanted her full attention as he aimed a spray of bullets at one side of the room, hosing down the human line, to kill as many people as possible. His goal was that no one would get out alive, including himself. As a little bonus, he hoped for the chance to hunt someone down in the bathroom. That's why he had attached the jagged hunting knife to his belt.

The energy in the room picked up. The one bolder, shadowy creature moved another step. It stayed hunched to the ground, its head tucked down. The rest of the mass pulsated, their combined whispers growing louder, along with coarse laughter. "Kill the bitch... kill the bitch dead...."

This boldness by the demons set Ohj on edge. His blood surged, and his hands itched to get around their slippery necks. He clenched his fists, trying to stay focused on Troy.

Eventually the knowledge that this might not be a simple marital spat, popped into a few customers' heads. Prayers went out, along with muffled crying. A couple of them tensed, getting ready to run for it. An ex-cop, originally first in line, inched past another customer. He had already crawled over two others. One more and he would be close enough to make a move for Troy's legs.

The manager came out from her office.

"Troy."

Hearing his name from behind startled Troy enough to take his finger off the trigger.

"Remember me from the company softball game? I'm Brenda." The manager stepped up closer. "Our team got creamed, but you and me, we didn't care because that got us faster into the dugout with the kegger."

She moved slowly, keeping her arms up. She was brave, and determined to stall until the police arrived, thinking they would swoop in to save them. "I know things have been rough, but you don't want to hurt anyone. There's a lot of scared people here. How about me, you, and Julia go to my office and talk it out?" She smiled faintly, then licked her lips and swallowed.

Troy snorted. "You don't think I wanna hurt anyone? Really?" Troy lunged forward and grabbed Julia with one arm, pulling her to his chest.

Now too close to the window, Julia's ogre ran for cover behind a customer. The other shadows grew thicker, spreading out. Whether the customers realized it or not, death had permeated the bank even before Troy had stepped into line.

Troy pointed the gun at Brenda. Without a pause, he fired off a couple rounds. One bullet hit the top of her head. Screams filled the air even after the bullets stopped. Blood fanned out on the white floor around the manager's body.

"That's for making her stay late all those nights to fill dumbass quotas," Troy said.

The tellers ducked under their shelves. Some froze, while others snaked down along the ground to group up with friends.

At movement from the ex-cop, Troy turned the gun and shot again, hitting the man in the back. He then pushed the blistering muzzle against Julia.

The smoky creatures began a low chanting, "Kill the fucking slut—kill the fucking bitch...."

Troy winced, cocking his head to the side as if he could hear them.

Ohj's chin dropped. Eyes on his shoes, he took a big breath and braced himself. He pushed himself through the window, sliding through the membrane of pressure, then breathed past the shock of cold. The demons who were smart enough to keep watch on him and not the humans, scattered, inking the area. The slower few yelped when they realized he was in their vicinity, disappearing before he could get his hands on them. With the air still vile and thick, he walked the room to make sure he was alone with the living.

At least now the scene could finish playing out without the heckling.

The customers he passed sent out a barrage of turmoil and information. The knowledge was so personal and complete, Ohj could address each person by name: answer the security questions for their bank accounts, and give Al, the suicide survivor, the exact moment his life derailed.

Breathing in spurts, John, the ex-cop, blinked before he lost focus due to the pain. After a recent job loss, his life meant so little to him that he preferred facing an Uzi than be branded a coward. Larry, the security guard, wasn't going to make a move to save anyone. Even though his demons were gone, he was still resigned to his fate. A tired man, he was relieved that all his problems were about to float away into what he hoped would be a nice, long sleep.

Sadness and desperation spread evenly through the lives on the floor. The broke and the financially comfortable, neither immune to hardships. Ohj wanted to touch them all, soothe their heartache. None of them deserved this death, he thought.

Ohj paused at Julia, beaten down and insecure after years of bullying. She adopted all responsibility for Troy's violence, believing this moment in time was her fault. He wished that everything would be alright: but it wouldn't be. These lives were about to be taken because of Troy's insanity. Even after these deaths, the pain would continue; inflicted on survivors who depended on their family member coming home.

Ohj walked over to stand behind Troy. The sleepless nights spent in preparation for this day left him even crazier. Ohj could smell sweat mixing with oily skin and fatigue. Years of anger and alcohol left Troy's arteries ballooning with pockets of sludge. Fresh adrenaline coursed through those same arteries, pushing hard on the weakened walls.

Sirens that seconds ago blared from a mile away, chirped off just outside. Ohj was glad, because the police would now stop a customer who was about to walk through the front doors, only to become another victim.

Troy still held Julia tight to his chest, breathing in her shampoo. He leaned against her, savoring the moment. He took a deep breath. And tensed.

Chapter Five

Ohj raised his hands to either side of Troy's head. Covering both ears with his palms, he pressed just slightly. Troy dropped the gun and staggered a step, away from Julia. He cradled his head just as Ohj had done; the blood gushing from between his fingers. His mouth went slack, and he fell to the floor.

Ohj went back to his witness room and reveled a moment at the physical relief. As the scene faded, he kept his back to the many guardians who had wandered into the bank. As far as they could know, he was there to witness the bank manager's death. The less they saw him the better.

There wouldn't be a long write-up on Troy. Not much to say. This was Troy's first serious crime, although it was good enough to make up for a lifetime. He went to his desk and ran his hand through his hair. He then started a book on Troy, who died of a stroke while trying to kill his wife.

His skin began to burn as he washed. He expected to find a pile of skin at his feet and was surprised at the few sparkles. The clear floor failed to cheer him—just the opposite. Fewer shimmering specks simply meant that the cells weren't regenerating fast enough to drop off. He continued to wash. A sporadic shine lingered dully, and he was beginning to peel in patches. Still, he couldn't be sure if it was the stress, or the harsh scrubbings that caused this new skin condition.

The trials kept coming at him. Plus, he just added another one. Events weren't supposed to be followed immediately by a trial. This wasn't a ping pong game. Seemed he was in court constantly, taking on cases two at a time.

He carried Troy's book. Again hand-delivering his account, exhausted, without a minute to rest.

Another trial was in session, so Ohj started to leave.

Red interrupted the session to point at Ohj half way down the aisle. "Don't you dare move."

Shoulders falling, Ohj continued to the front to wait his turn, taking a seat behind the prosecuting witness. As the defending guardian spoke up, Ohj thought about how much he wished he was by the lake. Disheartened, he looked up at the sky above the open room.

The witness in front of him was green; easily pegged by the attention he gave to the defense. No self-respecting witness bothers with the defense. Ohj kept his smile hidden, still wishing he were outside.

The human's guardian spoke loudly. "Peter served his neighborhood parish for fifty years, your Honor."

The courtroom waited for more from the defense, but after a minute of silence, Red gave his verdict.

As the sentence rang out over the tops of the spectators' heads, Ohj stood up to stretch.

"Don't leave yet, Ohj. We still have the one case for you. Seeing that you're in such a hurry, however, we'll make it fast so not to waste your time."

Ohj pat the new witness on the back as he took his place. "I'm in no hurry, your Honor. Please take all the time the court needs."

Red called Troy's name. After eyeing Ohj's thin book, he motioned for Troy's guardian to go first.

"Troy was a compassionate man," the guardian began. "He was always considerate of others...." The guardian didn't finish until the court heard all about the Dollywood trip Troy took his nephews and nieces on.

"He sounds wonderful," Ohj broke in, as Red shifted in his seat. "Any jealous rages you want to mention?"

"Did you start your testimony without my realizing?" Red interrupted. "I'm confused—was that written down?"

"No, but...."

Red waved his hand. "Read your testimony, Mr. Ohj. Please keep it to what you witnessed."

"I was prefacing, your honor. I apologize."

Red raised his hands. "Start."

Ohj had to balance thirty-nine, half-way decent years with one near-carnage. He ended his testimony with almost a plea. "Troy brought a Sub Machine Gun into a bank to kill twelve people, without care or mercy. If he hadn't died before he got the chance to murder, every one of those people would be dead instead of the one."

"Before this incident, sounds like the man lived a spotless life." Red regarded Ohj for a moment. "A first-time offender? You don't get many first-time offenders."

"First time offender or not, I would definitely not call him spotless," Ohj said, bringing the subject back onto his track. "And if you count all his victims, which I think the court should, he would be a twelve-time offender."

Red squinted. "My imagination isn't as good as yours, Mr. Ohj. I can't count twelve victims if they don't exist. However, one murder is serious, and punishable."

"He happened to die before he carried out the slaughter. His heart was full of twelve murders," Ohj insisted. He shut the book to point at Troy. "He died carrying twelve deaths in his heart. Thirteen, if you include his own suicide."

"So now I have to imagine his suicide?"

Troy's guardian interjected, "He died of natural causes, your honor. There was absolutely no suicide in the bank that day."

"Your honor, the suicide was every bit in his heart as if he'd completed it," Ohj said.

"As the twelve murders," Red said.

"Yes, your honor. He should be charged with all thirteen." Ohj refused to look at Troy's guardian.

Red glanced down at the book on his podium, then back up at Ohj. "The stakes are terribly high here, so please proceed cautiously. In your opinion, the court shouldn't show Troy mercy?"

Denying mercy was a dangerous game. Ohj breathed a moment, keeping his eyes on Red. His mind raced for the best answer. Red tilted his head to the side.

Ohj's words were just above a whisper. "Every soul is worth saving, your Honor."

Red rapped on his podium. "Mercy it is. Thank you for your insight, Ohj."

Outside, he watched as Troy and his guardian walked off, heads together as they discussed how he would serve his less-harsh sentence.

Another mishap on his conscious. He didn't even know Troy, he reminded himself. Had just met him. Lately, he barely had a chance to learn his clients' names. But now because of him, torturers and would-be murderers ran loose with the saints and the holy. That couldn't be good.

He drew back his foot to kick a rock but saw just in time that it had fur. He nudged the gerbil with his shoe, rousing it from its sleep, then sat down in its place on the edge of the road. From where he sat with his arms propped on his knees, sections of the path were visible as they wound around the lake. The swans were bright little specs. They floated along, keeping pace with the strolling bodies, while staying out of reach of any petting hands.

"Hey." Vincent dropped down next to him in the dirt. His wet hair and damp shirt implied that he'd just come from another trip to the witness' pools. "This place has a great view. I'll have to remember it."

Ohj felt like he had a new pet. He hoped Vincent was right when he said he was due for reassignment; no harm in adopting something with a short life span.

"Calmed down yet?" Vincent asked. He picked up a rock and threw it.

"What are you talking about?"

"You nailed my guy pretty hard. You just went at him like a train, then—wham! What did you hit him with—a brick? Would have ruined his little picnic, if not for all the love around. And he's dating now? What the heck is that all about?"

"Your guy?" Ohj turned to face him. "Do you mean Ronald Bass?"

Vincent leaned away from him and laughed. "That's exactly how you looked at *him*! Like a cartoon bull with steam shooting out of its nose."

Ohj's hands were already clenched by the time he got to his feet. He reached down, grabbed a fistful of Vincent's shirt, and yanked him up. With his other hand, he grabbed Vincent's throat. "Are you telling me you're that homicidal maniac's guardian? Because of you he got away with murder."

"Whoa—wait a minute. No one is madder than me at how things went down that day in court." Vincent's blue eyes grew large, but he didn't resist. "Come on, we're on the same side. I hated him as much as you, if not more. You honestly made my day when you slammed him. I only wish you'd done more damage; ripped that filthy smirk permanently off." His delicate face twisted into a grimace. "I wanted to tear him apart, limb from limb when they let him walk free." He took a breath to compose himself as he waited for Ohj to relax his grip.

Ohj let go of him but didn't step back. "I didn't see you at any of the murders, let alone at the trial."

"Yeah, I notice you don't pay much attention to us guardians. We aren't exactly on your radar."

Ohj wasn't satisfied. "In all those years, we should've crossed paths at least once."

"I didn't have the guts. You gotta be one sick bastard to watch that stuff—no offense. Bad enough I had to deal with him the other ninety-nine, point nine percent of the time. Imagine following him around minute to minute, guarding his disgusting soul. You got off lucky. After every murder, you got to walk away from that butcher."

Ohj dropped back down in the dirt, not responding when Vincent sat next to him again.

"You must know that I tried to get him to stop," Vincent said. "Did everything in my power to help those women—those poor souls, but I wasn't competition for his depravity. Nothing left for me to do but hang around the fringes. That's why I was so shocked when he made his so-called miraculous recovery. What a bunch of crap! I sure didn't buy into it, unlike your friend, the amazing, super-duper witness."

Ohj almost smiled. "He's anything but my friend."

"I can see you don't have much in common. He's not the brightest." He got up and put a hand on Ohj's shoulder. "So, we're still on the same team, right?"

Ohj shrugged. "I guess."

Vincent bent closer to Ohj's ear. "Good thing, cuz you're a scary sonofabitch. I don't want a fighting machine coming after me. Especially one who flings bricks."

Ohj stared ahead after Vincent left. That Ronald's guardian didn't believe in his transformation should have cheered him up—yet it was one more sign that the system was broken. A system he lived by. He pulled off his shoes. Same size as always, but they seemed to cut his toes off at the knuckle. He massaged the digits a bit to restore the circulation. Vincent didn't elaborate on what brought about Ronald's transformation. The guardian might be the only one who really knew. Although the technicalities hardly mattered anymore.

A bush rustled a few yards away. Even as he turned towards the noise, the plant seemed to lunge at him. Instinctively, he jumped to his feet just as a white lion leapt out. The lion charged, closing the ground between them. In full, bleached-white mane, its blue eyes shined as it stared at Ohj. Ohj relaxed and sat back down. Looming over him, the lion swished its tail from side to side in loud sweeps. Instead of taking a bite of the witness angel, the beast fell to its side as if shot dead.

"You're a long way from home, aren't you?" Ohj asked the lion.

A chunky fly buzzed around, swerving up and down as it dodged the lion's swatting tail. The lion yawned wide, showing off all its teeth and thick pink tongue. It put its head down, lying meekly at Ohj's burning feet like a sleek, snowy rug. Ohj wrestled with the idea to put the fur to good use.

"You're not safe here, you know. I see a big hairbow and painted claws in your future if you don't start moving."

Hearing someone behind him, he turned, half expecting Vincent back with more bad news. And dressed as his twin. Instead a different guardian passed him.

"Hello." The guardian glanced at him. "Nice cat." She moved down the hill so smoothly she appeared to fly, though her feet did touch the ground. Her dress fluttered behind her like shimmery wings. Underneath, a pearlescent material clung to her like a second skin. Rose pearl skin, and soft brown hair with strawberry highlights that sprang to life under the sun rays. She was truly stunning.

Ohj wasn't moved by beauty. Angels were beautiful, and none more than he. They all shared this trait: making envy as senseless as one puppy in the litter wishing they were as cute as another. What did move Ohj was the peace that flowed past along with her, like a river. Instantly it swept over him, soothing his overworked brain with a wave of calm.

Asia—her name popped into his head. He almost closed his eyes. The effect lingered only as long as her glance, leaving him cold again when she turned away. This tempted him to chase down that aura; discover her trick.

Instead he just sat, shoes in hand, watching her until she stopped. When she knelt beside the water, the birds rushed in for her attention. Instead of reaching out to pet a swan, she picked something up and put it in her pocket. It had to be small enough to fit. A feather? No, too weightless. A jewel or a stone maybe. Must be a very unusual object, for her to want to keep it. When he finally listened to his own thoughts, embarrassment cured his interest. Grateful he didn't have a habit of thinking out loud, he pulled his shoes on and stood up.

"You might have five minutes before the word spreads about you," Ohj told the lion, dead at his feet. "When that happens, you'll be hunted like you never have been before, and I won't be here to protect you from all the ribbons and braids in heaven."

Its snoring vibrated the ground as Ohj headed back to work.

Except for Vincent, guardians didn't seem to have a care in the world. If he got fired as a witness, maybe guarding wouldn't be such a bad reassignment. He'd be great at it; at least the protection part. Would give him the chance to kick some bully's ass. But if he got a Ronald for his person, that would be the first ass he'd kick. As much fun as it was to think about, he knew that each job was a calling. There was probably a very good reason why that guardian assignment never came to him.

Instead of going to the window, he lingered in his antechamber. He ran his hand over his granite bowl, more unpolished lump of stone than container. The etchings left jagged edges that could cut skin, encouraging one to only look at the tiny glittering scenes.

Above every other role, he was a warrior first. Built for battle, all muscle and fury. His greatest thrill came from destroying the enemy—cutting it into pieces and chopping off its head and/or heads. Never was he expected to show softness, let alone mercy. He always left his battles victorious and on fire, as if he'd basked in the sun all day. He thrived on staring down evil.

That one skill was the exact reason why he became a witness—to stare at evil. Unfortunately, it seemed, he still wanted to chop off its head. That was now the snag in an otherwise perfect plan.

The pale light from the window crossed the threshold into his antechamber. The scene opened to a basement.

Good. He was in the mood for a basement.

A pregnant woman lay tied to a cot. Almost full term, maybe a month shy, her exposed stomach showed every vein and stretch mark. She still had her skirt on, indicating that this wasn't a sexual attack—but Ohj knew that the second he saw Diana, standing over her with blue surgical gloves on.

Demons lined the walls, squeezing into the small space for the show. Ohj wanted to charge at them. Greedy for suffering and pain, they kept hollow eyes on the cot, hissing their hatred at the pretty human about to lose her life. So excited, they barely glanced at Ohj.

The pregnant woman, Stephanie, shivered not just from the fear of what was about to happen, but also from the cold that radiated off the cinderblock walls. The gag, a torn strip of beach towel, muffled her cries. She pulled at the rope tying her ankles and feet to the bed.

"Don't worry; I know what I'm doing. Your baby's gonna be fine," Diana said, as she poured rubbing alcohol over a scalpel. Her scalpel was makeshift from a set of permanently sharp knives she'd bought online. The set also included a great pair of scissors that would come in handy to cut the umbilical cord. Each piece of the set had its own place in the wooden block behind her on the old bookshelf.

Diana told the woman the truth—she did know what to do with the knife. She'd done this before with excellent results. The toddler from her last surgery sat upstairs, eating fruit loops. Diana was unable to bear her own children. Instead, nature provided her with the disposition to gain a large amount of weight around her middle, giving her a big, round belly often mistaken for a pregnancy. Nothing ruined her day faster than when asked when she was due. Ironically, that same belly became convenient when she needed to show up with a newborn.

"Got the baby's room already set up with Tessa's old crib and changing table. They're still like new. I redid the room with Elmo stickers, in case I'm having a boy." She laid out a clean baby blanket next to the woman on the cot, to set the new baby on. She smoothed out the warm, buttery yellow fabric. "I kinda like not knowing what I'm having."

"Cut her." The hissing began. The demons pushed in for a better look, while positioning themselves as far away from Ohj's window as they could get. Crouched down on their haunches, they elbowed each other for the safest vantage point. The entire group rocked back and forth in anticipation. One got jockeyed out in front, ending up dead center in Ohj's line of vision. Its skin had the texture of a dug-up corpse, and its filthy clothes stuck in places from the glue of open sores. It quickly clawed its way to the back again, ducking down behind the last row.

For Diana, this wasn't only about getting a baby, otherwise adoption would be a better solution. Even more than wanting a baby; she wanted to hurt pregnant women. She hated them and everything they represented. They paraded their bellies like trophies— as if they'd done anything other than screw some guy, to deserve the privilege.

She especially hated this one, whom she'd found at a Stater Brothers grocery store, parking her

Mercedes near Diana's minivan. Diana had followed her down the aisles, seething over her stylish maternity clothes, gel nails, and expensive high-heeled boots. What kind of pregnant woman grocery shops in high heels? Diana knew: one who lives a life of so much luxury that painful feet couldn't even begin to dim her comfort. Diana especially resented the large diamond ring on the woman's finger. She liked picturing the handsome, doting husband, waiting on the sofa for his wife to never come home. Probably had dinner laid out in front of a fire. This woman had everything that Diana didn't. For that insult, she was about to lose it all.

"Cut her —slice her open," one demon popped up to jeer. They leaned in as far as they could without falling on top of each other.

As a courtesy to the mother, Diana had offered her a couple shots of tequila to dull the pain. The fact that the mother refused the alcohol was her own fault, because this was going to hurt. And now that Tessa woke up from her nap, she didn't want to risk taking off the gag, so she wasn't going to offer the shots again.

With the scalpel rinsed clean, Diana refreshed her memory on what to do next by referring to the book opened on the cot. It was an old medical procedure book from the seventies that she'd found at a garage sale. Her hand shook a bit as she turned the page on home deliveries and emergency surgeries. If she screwed up, she could cut the baby too. She should have been brushing up the last few weeks, but she hadn't anticipated the opportunity to get a new baby quite so soon. It had just been four months since she decided to start trying again.

"Cut her already!" One demon rushed out from the line to scratch hard at the mother's leg with broken, dirty nails. The mother flinched, although no visible mark showed she had been touched. The demon scurried to the safety of the grumbling crowd. "You stupid bitch," Another snarled, taking a turn at the front, before losing nerve and retreating.

Ohj visually followed it to the rear. When it saw his attention, it squatted lower to the ground.

"Mommy, I'm hungry." Tessa knocked on the basement door, bolted from the inside.

"Put on Elmo. I'll be right up," Diana called. "I never get a minute," she said, turning to the woman on the cot. "It's not easy raising her alone, but I manage. Thank goodness I'm on a two-month vacay now. Sure gonna need it."

The vacation was courtesy of her maternity leave. She'd already exploited her big belly and dangerously high blood pressure. For the last couple months, she'd either gone home early, or taken long weekends.

One demon rushed in to jostle Diana's arm, knocking the scalpel out of her hand. The blade fell on the cot, barely missing Stephanie's exposed skin. Two more rushed in. One just to spit on the mother, while the other took a swipe at her belly.

Ohj stepped into the basement. "Now—" He choked on the next word, the stink of the group closing off his throat. "Get out!" he said, hoarsely.

The creatures ran, tumbling over one another to get away first. Ohj had his back to Diana but could hear the swish of alcohol as she re-cleaned the scalpel. He didn't have to turn to sense Stephanie. Married to Senator Tom Waters from the fourth district, she was used to jealousy from other women. And waiting for his wife in front of a cozy fire was the last place Senator Waters would be. At that moment, the senator happened to be flying over New York, with his assistant on his lap. What Stephanie also didn't know was, next year her husband would face a tax evasion charge and prison sentence.

Ohj turned toward the women. Arms relaxed at his side, he took in the scene.

The broken-down bookshelf behind Diana held all the basic drugstore medical supplies: peroxide, alcohol, and gauze, next to last season's homemade pickles. He could push the bookshelf on Diana, but then she and the cabinet would both land on the expectant mother. Diana could stab herself in the neck with the scalpel, but again, she might fall on top of the mother.

He took in the rest of the basement. It was tidy, giving him little to work with. A box of rat poison had possibilities—if he had the necessary days to sprinkle some into her morning coffee. A chain saw, a few boards leaning against a wall, a pink-handled screw driver. Any one of these provided opportunities. Last ditch—he could break a jar of pickles over her head.

Diana's pain came at him as he surveyed the room. A lifetime of rejection and anger screamed at him, demanding his attention. He turned away from her. With Diana gone, the police would finally piece together what had happened to the little girl upstairs. The little girl could then be reunited with her father and two older sisters. Ohj owed her that much, for standing by doing nothing while her mother was gutted and left for dead.

"Mommy let me in," Tessa called through the locked door, clasping the box of cereal with both hands. With her hands full, she started kicking with her foot. "I wanna come in."

"Chrissake. I'm coming," Diana yelled up. She put down her scalpel and went for the stairs.

An old Justin Timberlake song began playing in Diana's pocket. She stopped to pull out her phone. "Oh, I have to get this." She kept her back to the cot as she talked. "Hi, baby, what's up?" She put a foot on the bottom rung and leaned against the railing.

Next to her, Ohj heard the man's voice. Her boyfriend was about to become a father. She'd told him she was pregnant, but neither of them realized how far along she really was.

"I'm gonna have to pass on cooking tonight. Don't feel so good. Been getting pains all day, so, I think I'll just rest." She primed him to expect something, but nothing so big that he would panic and want to rush over. Ohj knew the man on the other end would need a lot more priming than that anyway.

Tessa started pounding on the door again. "Mommy, I spilled."

"Shit. Tessa made a mess. Gotta go. Call you later." She pushed the end button and yelled, "Tessa, dammit, I told you to watch Elmo."

Ohj waited until she ran up four of the wooden steps before sweeping one foot up in front of her. She swayed backwards, arms flailing out in midair. At the last second, she managed to throw herself forward and grab onto the rail. As she took a breath of relief, Ohj brushed her other foot. This time she wasn't as fast. On the way down, her face smacked against every stair, until she hit the concrete floor. She stayed there; face down and neck twisted, her legs bent beneath her.

Grimly, Ohj realized he had the experience necessary to know what to do next. He loosened the bindings around Stephanie's wrists and slid one hand out. She pulled out her other hand and undid her gag.

"Help," she screamed. "Someone, please help me."

"Mommy?" Tessa started crying.

Stephanie sat up stiffly. She tried to undo the knots at her ankles but fell back with a sharp pain. Ohj finished untying the rope for her and slid it onto the floor. So distracted with pain, she didn't notice the help. After a minute, she managed to get to her feet. Holding her stomach, she climbed over Diana, and started up the stairs.

Ohj looked down at Diana, unconscious, but still breathing. Maybe he wouldn't see her in court today after all. He hoped not.

He washed up after writing and left his work room. Diana walking up the stairs at that perfect time was pure luck. How many more accidents? How many spontaneous strokes? Or heart attacks—he hadn't used that one yet. That one was still available.

His shirt felt like it had been smeared with poison ivy then rinsed in sand. He pulled it off as he walked toward the lake. To catch the direct light, he held his arms out as he were about to fly. The sun touched down and attempted to kindle a flame. A spot on his back began to tingle, giving him hope. He willed it to grow, to spread to his sides and stomach. Behind him, he heard Red's swooshing garment. Without turning, he picked up his pace to outrun the judge. He aimed his steps over the grass and headed for the long path that stretched around the water. Red caught up quickly. Ohj was getting slow, becoming easy prey.

They walked a few feet in silence.

Red spoke first. "What is that—mange?"

Ohj slipped his shirt over his ears. After he got one arm through a sleeve, he changed his mind. Not wanting to discourage the spot on his back, he left the bulk of the shirt rolled up around his neck.

"What you need is a trip to the City. That'll cure you of whatever is going on with this," Red said, pointing at Ohj's chest. "Seriously, the City will do you good. You work too much."

"There's nothing wrong with me that a cigarette wouldn't fix. Thinking of taking up smoking, just as soon as I figure out where they sell them." He started getting itchy but resisted the urge to scratch. He rubbed his arm instead, hard.

"All right, I'm getting tired of dancing around your problem. Let's just get this out in the open." Red pulled him to a stop in the middle of the path. "You're still fuming that Ronald Bass got off on all charges. You can't let it go and it's turning you into a wreck. You haven't been the same since."

"Ronald who? That was ages ago—you're the one who can't let it go. Besides, how could I be mad? Did you hear him on the guitar? Crazy—how'd he pick that thing up so fast? Had me looking around for bongos. I was thinking of having him play at my next party."

"Your *next* party?" Red laughed.

Ohj started walking again so Red moved along with him. "Go ahead and deny it, Ohj, but it's eating you up and I can't figure out why. You said it wasn't your ego, so why are you taking this so personally?"

"I'm not. He didn't do anything to me; I'm not the one who got hurt. I just feel bad for all of his victims."

"Feel bad? I didn't even know you had feelings—you never let them out in public." Red walked faster, keeping up as Ohj tried to outpace him. "Okay—you're stuck on the notion that since he got off free, on your watch no less, you failed at getting retribution for the victims. If you'd paid more attention during the crimes, took better notes, the outcome would be different. Am I getting close? That's why you're upset, right? But do you know who else is upset that he's off free?" He leaned over into Ohj's face, almost tripping him. "Tell me—who else is upset that Ronald is free, Ohj?"

Ohj rolled his eyes. "I don't know, give me a hint —Bob?"

"No one, Ohj! No one else is upset." He threw his hands up. "Not his victims. Not their guardians. They're not mad. Not heaven itself. Only *you* are mad; furious in fact. You must let it go. It's not worth getting leprosy over."

"You don't think Ronald's victims are the least upset?" Ohj snorted. "Which one isn't? The one who lost her toes and fingertips, one at a time, to prolong his pleasure? How about the one he used the cattle prod on? I bet she's pretty pissed off."

"And I bet that they're all too busy loving paradise to give a shoot about Ronald Bass. Look around you—is anyone angry, or wants retaliation? Not counting you, of course."

Ohj didn't bother looking. He knew the happy faces would only annoy him. Vincent's words popped into his head: Ronald's guardian was irate—a perfect example. But bringing him into it would just prolong this immediate misery. More than winning an argument with Red, he needed a quick escape.

They stood blocking the path. A witness, in long shorts and a muscle shirt, read a hand-written account as he tried to walk around them. He jostled Ohj's arm, not bothering to apologize. He had a silvery sheen like what Ohj used to have. That warm, glowing silver Ohj now missed.

Red kept talking, taking advantage of the distraction. "The people here don't care how they got here, or who did what to them in life—who killed them, or lied to them, or stole their stupid money. They're just grateful to be here. There are no tears, or regrets. Can you point out even one person who's eaten up with righteous indignation? Again—present company excluded."

"I simply don't agree."

Ohj still watched the silver witness. The shine radiating off his arms and bare calves grew brighter by the second. An obsidian witness, with glass-smooth skin, joined him. Both glistened as they started a jog around the lake.

"Fine, you don't have to listen to me. We're surrounded by people. Let's ask a random victim how they feel now." Red ran a few feet to a person walking with a guardian and a black lab. He grabbed the man by the arm and pulled him over to Ohj.

The dog ran alongside the man, refusing to break contact with his owner's jeans.

"Hold on, there. I'm comin'." The person smiled broadly. He waved his guardian over to follow. "This is crazy. What's goin' on here?" The three came to a stop in front of Ohj.

New at death, the man had just settled in to the country. He not only still wore the same gray shaggy beard he had when alive, but also the plaid shirt and John Deere belt buckle. The shirt had all the faded comfort of a favorite, creating the illusion that at that minute he'd climbed off his combine to take a walk around the lake. The grubbiness of the dog's pink and white bandana, permanently knotted around her neck, hinted that she too came as she was.

Red positioned the person to face Ohj, who immediately took a step back. "Young man," Red started, with a charming wink. "Settle a bet between us: do you have any bad thoughts toward the individual responsible for your death?"

"Don't know. Who, the doctor? Nah—he did his best. I shouldn't have ignored all the weird lookin' moles that started popping up." He stared at Ohj's arms as he spoke. "My wife kept at me to go see the doctor, go see the doctor...."

Ohj's lip curled as he pushed his arm through a sleeve and pulled the shirt over his stomach.

The farmer scratched the top of the dog's head. "...When I finally did get to the doctor, he told me to wear sunscreen and hats bigger than my cap, but I didn't. Probably too late by then anyway."

"Thank you." Red eased the farmer back along his way, and whispered to Ohj, "Give me another minute."

Two women walked toward them. "Here we go." Red stepped up to block their way. "Ladies, quick question: what do you think about your death? Do you wish your death had more meaning—let me clarify—were you wronged? Do you wish *you* could punish the wrong-doer more harshly?"

"Um, no," one woman said, shrugging. "I had diabetes. The only one I could punish is the one who fried up all those donuts I ate." She and her friend started laughing. "Am I right?"

Ohj sighed and reached under his sleeve to scratch at a spot above his elbow. He stopped when he realized what he was doing. The silver flecks under his fingernails verified that he'd just scratched off a square of good skin. He raised his sleeve and twisted his arm to see if any silver was left. The spot looked dull. He glared at Red.

Red had turned to the next woman. Ohj focused over the top of her head, at the two jogging witnesses to check if they were even shinier by then. They were. As they raced along, their glowing reflections bobbed in the water beside them as if on leashes.

"I was born with spina bifida. Spent all my life in a chair, watching all the other kids running and playing. Now I can dance and spin all...."

"Sorry for your loss," Red interrupted. He put an arm around Ohj's shoulders and led him away. "You get the message."

He kept talking as they walked up the grass, leading Ohj farther from the lake where the best sunshine fell. "It doesn't matter how a person dies. It only matters how they lived. And there is a reason why 'vengeance is mine..., sayeth the Lord,'" he said, in his deep court-appointed voice. Ohj cringed, but Red's arm weighed down his shoulders, preventing an escape. "It takes a great burden off people. No one has to hold a grudge, or stress about getting their revenge. Everyone can die in peace. Then, even though no one else cares—vengeance is still His."

"And the family that's left behind to deal with the horrible way they lost their loved one? They aren't in peace. They still want their vengeance."

"And then, they don't," Red countered. He walked ahead when Ohj stopped. "What a wonderful gift—not to have to hang onto all that pain." His voice got louder as he walked away, until eventually he was yelling. "We are in paradise, Ohj. You're the only one who's mad about that."

Frowning, Ohj stared at the judge's back. Just before Red disappeared, Ohj shouted to him, "Hey, it's all rainbows and sunshine for me from now on. And I promise to start chasing my inner unicorn." He then added more quietly, "Hopefully when I find it, it won't be in someone's basement with electrodes attached to its nipples."

A guardian passed by. "Ewww."

Ohj wished he had a mirror to check his back. One way Red's lecture did him good—this was the longest he'd been out in the sun in what seemed like years. Even if he was forced to take in all his sustenance through the one undamaged spot, the last several minutes had to do him some good. And if a little sun did him good, then a lot more would do him better. He picked up a smooth rock to skip across the water. As he let the missile fly, a sharp pain shot up his arm. The rock jumped once then sank.

Forget Ronald and revenge, he had more important things to think about, like surviving despite losing his outer layer of skin. As he walked, he kept close to the water to catch whatever sun reflections bounced off the surface. He breathed deeply, sucking the warm air all the way to the depths of his lungs, just in case he hid some silver internally. Twice he stopped, turned his face up and looked directly into the round flame burning hot in the sky. Both times he had to look back down, and blink away the pain.

Eyes watering, he continued onward, instead now he searched the hill for a small wooden hut: a landmark to the shortcut that led back up to the road. He was ready to go home.

The white lion lay stretched out at the base of huge willow. When Ohj passed the tree, the beast lifted its enormous snowy head. Glowing, blue-ice eyes regarded Ohj carefully. The animal slowly dragged itself to its feet, using agonizing effort, as if pulling free of a tar pit. Then in one incredible leap of energy, the cat jumped down on to the path next to Ohj.

The big cat kept up Ohj's pace, swishing its tail at its pet fly that still hovered just out of reach. Together, the three passed another tree. The lion looked longingly at the moss and leaves cushioning the base. Ohj expected it to wander off and drop down for another nap. Instead, it continued to move along with him.

Ohj kept eyeing the beast. Thick muscles undulated with every step, swaying along with the back that almost reached Ohj's hip. White fluff couldn't quite conceal the sharp claws sticking out of its gigantic front paws.

"This is a little weird. You aren't waiting for a chance to eat me, are you?"

The hut Ohj sought after finally came into view. Before Ohj took another step, the lion came to a standstill. Ohj stopped too, looking down at the beast. Ears twitching, the lion cocked its head to the side. This time Ohj heard the shrill whistle, coming from some distance. The lion turned, and with renewed vigor, bolted straight up the hill. The ear-piercing whistle sounded again, as if someone grew impatient with the animal's lack of progress.

Ohj peered up through the trees but saw nothing. He moved to catch up, grabbing onto shrubbery to haul himself faster. He could just make out the lion's hind legs pumping at the dirt above. Towards the top, the lion began to gallop, gaining momentum for those last steep yards. The lion made it over the crest of the hill with Ohj still far behind. Ohj ran to close the distance, clambering up to the edge on his hands and knees.

Two armed soldiers stood on either side of a small chamber. They made way for the lion to cross the threshold between them.

There was no chamber there before. Ohj passed the spot several times a day; nothing stood there before. The building was taller than the soldiers and not much wider than his own witness room. Though new, it was solid: built of age-old granite.

Fascinated by this new construction and who lived inside, Ohj jumped to his feet. The soldiers didn't say a word. They remained standing at the sides of the entrance: the same stance as when the lion passed.

Unable to see anything past the doorway, despite the large opening in the front, Ohj sprinted to join the lion. Once at the entrance, he leapt inside—and hit a wall.

Chapter Six

The impact threw him backwards. He somersaulted off the edge of the hill, and onto his stomach. As he slid down, he raked at the ground with both hands, grabbing blindly for exposed tree roots or bushes to slow himself. Once the skidding stopped, he got up on his knees. His shirt was pushed up to his chest, exposing a scraped stomach. He pressed on his nose—it clicked as the cartilage underneath readjusted, and his front teeth felt loose from the initial hit. He pushed himself up off his knees and went back up the hill. When he got close to the top, instead of bounding up and over like a German shepherd, he used a little more caution: crawling until he could see.

The soldiers were gone. The chamber was gone. He got to his feet and faced only the road that led to the witness rooms. He walked through the space where the chamber had just been, his steps unobstructed: no invisible wall knocked him back.

Eyes to the ground, he turned a full circle, looking for any marks in the dirt. In case the lion crouched nearby, he whistled, imitating the signal he'd heard before. Nothing.

Laughter and chatter warned him of approaching guardians. He ignored them. With his fingers in his mouth, he tried another whistle, this time in the opposite direction. Soon, round-bodied males and females surrounded him on all sides.

The Botticellis—a well-earned name he gave to this large group ages before—scantily clad in flowing gowns. The guardian's skirts opened to show off fleshy knees and calves. Long curly hair and flowing sash waistbands flew in all directions. Laughter chimed throughout. Filmy material brushed Ohj's arms as the guardians strolled around him, like he was a puddle to avoid. Ohj blinked, absently wiping at the pebbles still embedded in his shirt.

The guardians incorporated a few humans into their enthusiastic clique. A history teacher, waving a long scarf, held the hand of a librarian in a leaf headband. Ohj checked either side of him for the fastest route out of the crowd. He pulled his shoulders in close to his body, so not to touch every one of them that passed. A canopy of perfume hung overhead, incorporating him, until he too became a part of their renaissance party. He inched sideways as best he could. He was more than half way through when everyone froze in place. It had started to rain.

The Botticellis looked up as glittery drops cascaded down from the cloudless sky. Each drop reflected a sliver of sunlight, falling like a shining crystal. From the ground, the air above them appeared to explode with tiny fire crackers. The

Botticellis stretched up their hands to catch the precious droplets. In their excitement, they forgot to let Ohj out of the circle. A golden Pomeranian, hair trimmed to resemble a tiny bear, poked its head out of the librarian's bodice. The dog lunged to snap at Ohj when he got too close.

They filled in around him, syrup-thick, blocking all his exits. Wet glitter bounced off his hair and ran down his shoulders. A guardian caught a crystal on her tongue. The rest joined in, jumping up in random spurts. Jostled, Ohj searched for a weak spot in the procession to slip out through. Soon he found one, between an actor and a painter. He plowed through, bursting free just as the rain started to slow. The ahhs of disappointment left him unmoved, until he realized his escape route put him in the direct path of the storm. The Botticellis no longer danced beneath the beautiful showers, but two feet away, the crystal drops still fell on Ohj.

He moved fast, without daring to look behind. The glitter hit him face on and permeated his lungs with every breath. Only after he made it to his work room, did he stop to shake the crystals out of his hair. He pulled his shirt to his nose and groaned. The fabric smelled like a funeral home.

Ohj couldn't relax, even when he stood safely at his window, watching a couple stroll through a park. The disappearing chamber was something new to him. He had a strong hunch that it was a window of a different sort. He'd never considered that there might be different kinds of windows—maybe ones that watched him? Before, the possibility was irrelevant. Now, it was too dangerous not to consider. If Ohj had a wall with a panoramic view, what would a High

Witness have? A chamber? One that opened anywhere, including at the top of a hill?

The young couple smiled as they walked towards a playground, enjoying the fresh, beautiful October day.

What did the High Witness hope to see, parked across from the witness rooms? And why couldn't those soldiers stop him from running at it breakneck? A little warning would have been nice. They didn't even try to slow him down. If only he got into that building along with the lion, he might have all his questions answered. He should have run faster, dove harder. If he got another chance, he would do just that. Probably break his neck, but it would be worth it. He pushed on his nose to check if the bones had reset yet.

The couple in the window continued their stroll, circling a sandy area loaded with swings and monkey bars. Squeals filled the air, as a cacophony of children dumped their excess adrenaline on the playground equipment.

Whether he was distracted by outside influences or not, he had to stop acting as reckless as a schoolboy. Time to behave—he was being watched. More offense, less defense. Most importantly, his bad guys had to stop dying on him. Do the job at hand like a million times before, he told himself. How hard could it be?

Fluffy clouds blocked the sun's harsher light, leaving only crisp air and swaying brown leaves. The humans took advantage of the air before the Illinois' winter snowed them in. At first Ohj ignored the demons. They followed the couple loosely, limping along. Ohj also stayed with the couple, easily outpacing the demons.

Recently comfortable with the feel of each other's hand, the couple wandered onto a jogging trail that telescoped off the main park. Jeff just graduated with a master's degree in business, and had that week landed a job with Nike. Mandy studied finance, due to graduate in the spring; already a prime target for head hunters. They didn't come from money, were regular shoppers at thrift stores, and they weren't especially attractive as far as humans go. But they smelled of hope: the most beautiful of perfumes.

Ohj glanced in both directions. More demons waited down the trail ahead of them, boxing the young couple in. They drooled excitedly. Even before the trail led through an area of bushes, Ohj identified their attacker. Art crouched behind the junipers, listening for good candidates to come his way. In gray sweatshirt and baseball cap, he waited for the couple to get closer. As soon as they cleared the bush, he jumped out from behind and shoved his gun into Jeff's back.

"Get behind the bushes."

Mandy looked behind her. "Oh my God. Oh my God." She grabbed onto Jeff's arm.

Art pushed her forward when she didn't move. She stumbled stiffly toward the bushes, letting go of Jeff.

Jeff put his hands up. "No problem. We'll give you whatever you want."

"Good. Start with your wallets." Art ran his eyes over the pair. No jewelry or watches. "And your phones." He nodded in approval at Jeff's brand-new iPhone. Same time, he double-checked the playground. At this angle, the park was still in view, though no one paid any attention. A man unfolded an easy-up awning, as his wife hauled a box with a pink and purple piñata balanced on top. Two kids wearing birthday tiaras ran circles around them.

"Back more," Art said, pointing with his gun to a cluster of trees.

The pair went in deeper until they were completely out of view from the rest of the park. Art held the gun to Jeff's face. Ohj knew Jeff was about to die. And once Jeff was gone, Mandy would be at Art's mercy. Ohj also knew that Art had no mercy.

The demons closed in.

A being with bare feet and rotting skin that showed behind the holes in his feudal leggings, stood scarcely one foot from the window. Never had Ohj seen a demon come this close to his room.

Ohj stepped out to claim the scene. The demon took a couple hops back, giving up little of his space. One arm dangled loosely from the demon's body, hanging not so much from a thread of skin, but from his puffy sleeve. Ohj looked around slowly at the beings. Most of the creatures bore putrid stumps and permanently oozing wounds, possibly from his own hand. Even the best of them was tattered, no more than rags suspended off the ground.

How easy to knock them over; cut them down. One slithered closer to him, then jumped backwards again, almost falling from the effort. A being in a yellowed uniform nodded in Jeff's direction. Two moved in to take a swipe at the young man. They danced back, staying just beyond Ohj's reach, daring him to give chase. They smiled coyly like they all played a game. Only the rage burning in their eyes gave up how serious they were. They were taunting him, trying to lure him away from the couple.

"Stupid," Ohj hissed. Though he would never admit it, the sight of those filthy hands on this young pair did make him want to give chase and risk the job at hand. How badly he wanted to, was something he guarded behind a tight smile.

"Hurry with it," a large demon whispered at Art. He limped up closer to stand near Mandy. One of his legs was shorter than the other and turned inward at the ankle. He blinked continually, one of his lids closing over an empty socket. "You wanna screw her, don't you? Quick before anyone comes."

Art shoved the muzzle of the gun into Jeff's mouth. Terrified, Jeff worried he would vomit, and cause the gun to go off. He panted shallowly through his nose, trying not to taste the tang of the dirty metal pressing down his tongue.

Art glanced at Mandy from the corner of his eye. "You don't move. You don't scream."

"Shoot him! Do it!" the same demon shrieked. "She's ready for you. Scared and wet. Just the way you like 'em." His head twitched from the constant eye spasms.

Ohj frowned at the couple. Both shook with fear; their beautiful human scent gone. They now reeked of fright. About to die at Art's hand, their last few breaths filled with hatred and pungent decay of demons. Ohj was not going to stop their deaths: determined to do his job. But in a few short minutes, some people would find the path. If he could buy the couple a little time, he might spare Mandy at least the pain of rape.

"Check out this jackass. He doesn't have the balls for it." A demon shoved his slashed face into Art's. "Quit bein' a pussy and blow his melon head off."

"Shit! Afterwards, I'll even hold her down for you," one demon screeched, holding up a stump of a hand.

"Hold her down for me too. I'll poke her," Another demon shouted.

"I'll poke the other one too, don't care if he's breathin' or not." Four demons began to circle. Ohj felt one brush his back, but didn't dare turn away from Art.

"I'll cram a stick so far up his arse...." A demon next to Art promised.

"Step back before I rip off your other arm," Ohj told the demon. The demon stepped back, tripping over another crowding in from behind.

A hawk, feathers roughed up, swooped down from a tree. Ohj saw the movement from the corner of his eye but paid little attention. He looked up just as the hawk dove at his head. Instinctively, he leaned out of the way of the talons. The demonic group roared.

More birds gathered, rustling the trees harder than the soft breeze. A demon jumped up and whooped at the trees. A few birds flew out, rushing at Ohj before settling on the tree directly behind him. Just inches away, he felt the birds' flutters on the back of his neck. The birds couldn't harm him. His own growing temper was a much bigger threat.

The couple hadn't moved. Jeff still stood, patiently waiting for his head to get blown off. Ohj took hold of the barrel of Art's gun with one hand, as if to help the human steady it.

Art pulled the trigger. The gun clicked half-heartedly. All the demons stopped moving to focus on the gun still in Jeff's mouth. As the demons leaned in, Art pulled the trigger again. Nothing happened, so he yanked the pistol back, cracking Jeff's two front teeth.

Instead of running, kicking out, or even punching their attacker, Mandy and Jeff stood frozen as Art inspected the gun. Seeing that the gun was still fully loaded, Art shoved it into Jeff's sweater, right over his breast bone. He squeezed the trigger. It jammed for the third time.

Five bicyclists headed towards the path. Still on the other side of the grounds, they would ride up on the robbery in a matter of seconds.

Art turned the gun around to double check the safety. He inspected the little lever up close, then from a few inches away, turning the gun over in his hands. It went off. A bullet tore sideways through his neck ripping open the skin and muscle and nicking an artery. He fell forward onto his knees. Blood sprayed Jeff and Mandy, showering their faces and clothes.

That made them run.

The birds left the trees in a wild storm of flapping wings.

Ohj started coughing, as if his own airway was filled with torn skin and blood. Back in his room he still held onto his neck. The park was still lit up in his window. Art was rolled into a ball on the dirt, choking on his last breaths. The demons squeezed in to watch. The wound was too severe for Art to survive long. Not even his guardian could get someone to him fast enough, although that being was nowhere to be seen. Covered in blood, Jeff and Mandy quickly got attention. People surrounded the pair, trying to figure out which was hurt the worst.

Ohj had barely touched the gun—definitely wasn't touching it when it went off. Should he write that down? Explain to the court that he had no idea why Art pulled the trigger when he did. In his own defense; why on earth would Art pull the trigger while looking down the barrel?

He stank, so tried not to breathe as he wrote. Unable to finish fast enough, he began stripping off his fouled clothes the second he stood up. Even before his shirt made it off, he knew the one healthy spot on his back was gone.

The mint stung. He flinched from every drop that hit his skin, let alone the handfuls necessary to effectively clean all the contamination. Ignoring the stack of clean towels, he stood naked in the cool air to dry, then gingerly redressed. The material clung to every sore inch of his battered skin. When he pulled the front away from his chest to ease the contact, the fabric raked his back. He slid his feet into his shoes slowly, feeling every raw spot.

He grabbed Art's book. The robber had still been alive when his window closed, but barely. Good chance he'd beat Ohj to Red's courtroom.

In the hall, the Viking stomped towards him. His dreadlocks were pulled back in a ponytail, and his leather vest displayed tarnished armbands clamped above his elbows. They had to turn sideways to pass each other. The Viking walked passed Ohj's room and continued down towards the end of the hall. Ohj made a mental note to find out who occupied the rooms on either side of him. Might be a good idea to befriend those witnesses, or least keep tabs on them.

Outside, the air still smelled of rain. Art's book in hand, he decided to risk the park to get some sun. He stepped around a couple of guardians. One tried to hand him a flower. He pretended not to notice as the daisy bounced off his arm. The flower joined three others like it on the ground.

He sat down in his old spot and squinted past the piercing light floating in the water. The swans grew more fluorescent by the day. He wondered what they were eating. He pivoted to another direction, so the neon white would scald just the corners of his eyes. He pushed up his sleeves, to let his arms breathe. A few shiny stragglers above his elbows persevered, but without the necessary numbers, their work was futile.

He rolled his pants up past his knees. His legs seemed to shine a bit more than his arms. If this didn't work, he might have to strip naked to uncover all hidden silver.

Three bright-colored balls floated over, their reflection unmistakable in the water below. Two were horizontally striped: red and yellow, blue and lime. The third was a kaleidoscope of iridescent shards that shifted with the movement. All three were mirrored in the lake. The hot air balloons drifted over, carrying baskets filled with waving people. A whooshing sound, each time a fire sent up a gush of hot air, accompanied the slow progress.

Looking up pinched Ohj's neck, so he focused back on the water.

In the watery reflection, a tiny figure perched on the brim of one of the baskets. Soon all three baskets wobbled as shadowed figures climbed out to balance on the edges. The person dropped straight down in a freefall, making a nosedive for the lake.

A growing shadow fell on Ohj. He jerked his head up just as the figure threw out their arms to let loose fabric sails. Catching a wind, the sails straightened out the fall before the person hit the water. Two more jumped, their shadows striking Ohj before golden red and green arm-sails picked them back up. The wind carried them all away, their sails as bright as the balloons.

The sky soon filled with flyers, dipping and weaving around each other and over Ohj before the wind led them away. With a loud whoosh, the balloons fired up to follow.

Ohj realized he was breathing hard. He put his head down on his bare knees and waited to catch his breath.

He left his pant legs rolled up as he walked to the court steps. Not until he was standing in front of Red's podium did he remember to push them back down to his ankles.

Red called Art forward to stand before the court.

Ohj kept his eyes down as he read, fully immersed in the words. "Art held up a young couple at gunpoint...." His details included the beautiful day, the crowd outside the crime scene, as well as the three times he pulled the trigger point blank on Jeff. "...And in doing so, accidently shot himself with his own weapon."

"Why is he in chains?" Red asked.

Ohj came to. "What?"

"He's guilty of attempted robbery. Why is he in chains? Usually, they're reserved for the more serious offenders." Red responded.

Ohj stared at the words in the book. "What is so remarkable about Art, and why he absolutely requires those chains, is that a large number of evil spirits congregated around him. These spirits were abnormally aggressive. He had to work for many years to gather such a group, and although young in his crime spree, I believe this particular demonic crowd is proof that Art is a danger to those around him."

Art lay on the floor weeping. Red finally waved at his guardian to start with the defense. Sadly, for Art, his guardian's defense was even shorter than Ohj's.

"Art wasn't a bad guy...," he began, the defense losing steam right afterwards.

Ohj suspected that the reason the defense was short was probably because the guardian couldn't stand Art's repulsive escort. The guardian hardly knew his ward. So, the best of Art's defense ended with his ninth birthday. That was the day Art saved a puppy from drowning in a reservoir. The guardian didn't tell the court what happened to that same dog after Art turned ten.

The guardian finished with a cough.

Red's gaze passed from the guardian, to Ohj, then down at Art. This wasn't about whose case was stronger, but whose wasn't weaker. And because Ohj's accounts were the shortest, Art got off easy. Banned from the City and sentenced to a modest existence.

Red released him to his guardian, who sighed loudly. The guardian frowned as he led the human off to his life everlasting.

In a twist of fate, Art's death in life spared him a life in hell. With no City privileges, Art would be hanging around the country. Ohj rolled his eyes. He had just found a new victim to protect: his own.

In no mood for swans, or attacking parasailers, Ohj walked back to work. He shook his head. How was he supposed to rescue these clumsy humans? Apply pressure to their wounds? CPR until the paramedics arrive?

In the hallway outside his rooms, Ohj stopped his cleaner. He blocked the cleaner's path, then without warning, pulled his white shirt up over his stomach. "Seems the mint in the water is messing with my skin." Ohj turned a slow 360 to show him. "Honestly, been using the mint for a long time. I'm ready for a change anyway."

Arms full of wet washcloths and dirty clothes, the cleaner had to look up to survey Ohj's exposed back as it passed by. The skin was mottled; peeling areas exposed a mysterious gray layer underneath. A few scratched spots were crusted over. The cleaner stepped back a step. "Want me to add some Penicillin?"

"No—but that was funny. It's just a little irritated. Can you can dig up something other than mint. Something soothing and refreshing?"

"Lemon?"

Ohj's skin twitched. "I think we're going in the wrong direction. What does the guy next door use?"

"Nothing."

"And on the other side?"

"Sometimes might burn incense, I think. Or maybe a scented candle?"

"I see."

The cleaner's eyes hovered over Ohj's scabs a minute. "Want me to get something now?"

Ohj contemplated the fresh bowl of the stinging mint on his table. The offer tempted him, but the sound of his window warming up in the next room, traveled all the way into the hallway. He let the cleaner pass by. "No, but definitely next time. Thanks...."

He pulled his shirt down and stretched on the neckline until it gave an extra inch. After shutting both doors, he leaned a book against each; part barrier, part alarm. As he stood in front of the window, he held his shirt out away from his chest and stomach.

The smoke of burning cedar and oak filled Ohj's nostrils. A blazing fire glowed in the two-sided fireplace that connected the living room to the game room. No scent of rotting filth. He surveyed the walls of the room. No demons lurked; not even a smudge greasing the corners. Ohj quickly realized why: Asia. The angel with the aura stood at the far end of the room, a shine around her like a light bulb holding off nightfall.

The guardian was as beautiful as he remembered. Skin glowing a rich, pearlescent rose, eyes clear as amber glass. Even from behind the window, he felt the warmth radiating from her. Her presence stunned him, making him wonder if the window opened too early, or even accidentally. A guardian in the room at this time?

A woman, Susan, moved her head out of range of a rebar rod, almost tripping over the brick hearth.

She lived in her boyfriend's house, with high ceilings that echoed every whack from the rebar he swung.

Susan grabbed the pole with both hands. "Please, Baby. You know I wouldn't leave you. I'm staying."

"I don't give a shit what you do." Doug's words were slurred from gin. The alcohol did little to soften his ever-present anger. And finding her packed suitcase had little to do with the fact that he had a steel bar and wanted to hit something with it.

In the foyer, Doug's assistant heard Susan's pleas. She stood around the corner, Bluetooth in her ear, a laundry bag for the cleaners in her arms. She had to step over Susan's bulging suitcase to get to her keys on the side table. When the assistant kept walking towards the front door. Asia left her ward to follow.

"You need to help," Asia told the assistant very clearly. "Make some noise. Let him know you're here and aware of the beating."

A muffled thump came from the living room. Susan cried out; then cried out again. The assistant looked over her shoulder at the doorway to the room where her boss yelled a string of obscenities at his girlfriend. She paused with her hand on the door knob.

Asia also reached for the knob, covering the assistant's hand with her own. "Susan needs your help. You know in your heart that he will kill her. Go back in and help her."

Eyes down, the woman crept out the door. She carefully shut it behind her to make as little noise as possible.

Asia followed the assistant to her car, parked at the front of the circular driveway. She pleaded with the assistant from outside the driver's window. "Please. Ignoring this won't keep you safe." The assistant started the engine, with Asia still begging. "You will be next. You have to intervene now; for your own sake, if not for Susan's."

The Audi tore down the driveway with the volume cranked up on the playlist.

Asia ran to a gardener kneeling in the dirt at the side of the porch. "Go help or call the police."

Ohj knew there was no way this man was going to call the police, even though he too heard Susan's cries. He trusted the police even less than he trusted his employer. As Ohj expected, the gardener stayed hunched over the broken sprinkler. By the time Asia returned to the living room, Susan cowered in the corner. Bleeding welts covered both forearms like stripes. Her cheek had a cut where the sharp tip of the bar sliced her skin.

Asia got in between them to reason with Doug. "You're upset—you aren't thinking clearly." Her words were soft, said almost lovingly, like a mother who was trying to put a frustrated child down for a nap. She laid her hand on his arm. "Put the bar down and take a breath. You've done enough damage. A game is on in the other room. Get some chips—call for pizza. Everything will be better then."

Doug's face remained an angry mask. Had he heard the words or sensed the soft touch of the angel, he didn't show it. Doug raised the bar to hit Susan again. He acted on his own—no demons to coach him; their prodding unnecessary.

Ohj's mouth dropped open from surprise. How could a human so close to this rare being not be moved, even by the slightest? Ohj himself, was humbled by her. Even demons recognized Asia for what she was, staying far away so not to get burnt by her bright shadow.

But not this human. In all her glory, she pleaded with this man to show basic human compassion—a natural human trait. Yet he couldn't dredge up the smallest amount of mercy.

Comfortable with his choice, Doug continued to rant. "After everything I've given you, you repay me like this?"

Giving up on his conscience, Asia went to soften the next blow instead. The bar landed weakly on Susan's arm. Doug tried the shot again. When the swing fractured Susan's leg, Asia went to the ground with her.

Asia's hair fell over the wounded woman in brown waves. She caressed Susan's forehead, trying to comfort despite the pain. The pipe came down on Susan's stomach. The impact rocked the guardian along with the woman.

Asia looked up at Ohj. This was the first time she acknowledged him, though she had to know he was there the second the window opened. As if by ignoring him, she could fight the inevitable. Tears soaked her cheeks, but she didn't talk to him. There was nothing to say. Plead with him to save Susan? She could save her, herself. They both knew the outcome. Ohj wasn't there by accident. He was there to witness the last beating this woman would take.

Ohj itched to grab the pipe and smash the boyfriend's face with it.

121

Asia glanced again at Ohj when he walked through his window.

Doug screamed down at woman on the floor. "Who the hell do you think you are? You're nothing but trailer trash, whoring your way into my house. Now you think you can just leave? You filthy whore."

"I'm sorry," Susan cried. "I thought you were tired of me. I was getting out of your way."

The pipe came down, drawing out another scream.

Ohj decided he would tear the man's arms off. He got down on his knees across from Asia. "Let me do my job," he said softly. "Go now."

The rebar flew past Ohj's ear to hit Susan's shoulder. She screamed and brought her hand up to the spot. Her hand shook, along with her bruised body. Asia also touched the spot, then tried to hold Susan tight enough to stop the trembling.

"She shouldn't die so soon. Not with such violence." Asia ran her hand over Susan's hair. "You don't know her like I do. She's so loving. Choosing this man was her only mistake."

The rebar came down again. Ohj clenched his fists and slapped it away before it made contact. "Go. Now. Let me do this. This is what I'm here for."

"Shhh…. It's almost over," Asia murmured into the woman's ear. She turned to Ohj and shook her head.

Susan quit crying out. Instead, she swallowed hard when the rod swooshed past her eyes, barely missing her.

"Go." Ohj put his hand up to deflect another blow. The bar bounced away, almost flying out of Doug's hands. "I can help her. Leave before it's too late. Before too much damage is done." He blocked another blow, easily, with a wave of his hand.

Doug looked at the rod that seemed to have a life of its own. He twirled it around to reposition the thin bar.

"I won't leave her," Asia said.

The next blow came down on Susan's skull. "You're not so brave now, are you bitch?"

It was over. Ohj let his head drop.

Not realizing she had died, Doug kept swinging the bar, hitting the body on the ground repeatedly. Susan and her guardian didn't stay. Ohj caught a glimpse of Asia as she left: unsmiling, without the contented expression of a guardian escorting someone to paradise. No welcome-home party. She looked tired and desperately sad.

Ohj failed her. He failed when he did his job, and he failed when he didn't. He almost had to crawl back to his room.

As he wrote up Doug's account, he realized he hadn't paid attention to the details. How many times did Doug hit her? What exactly did he say? Ohj paid more attention to the guardian. He barely had enough information to fill out the book, yet such a violent crime would normally take a large volume. He hoped no one would ask if there were any other people in the house, because he didn't notice. At this rate, Doug would get a weak sentence, just because of Ohj's lack of detail.

He stripped the clothes off his raw body. He picked up a wet cloth, only to put it back down on its pile. Instead, he smoothed a little water over his arm. Gingerly, he took another handful and rolled it over his shoulder and biceps. Lastly, he dribbled the water on his stomach and legs. Each drop burned like acid. The painful process forced him to concentrate on the rite of true purification, as his defiled skin was slowly disinfected, inch by inch.

He looked at the fresh clothes as he stood drying. The pile seemed heavy, abrasive. A sleeveless shirt and shorts suddenly appealed to him. But he also realized the long sleeves and pants offered his body concealment, if not comfort. He lifted his foot for a closer look. A painful, hot patch had started to ache with each step. Before putting the shoe on he stuck his hand in to stretch it out from the inside. A couple seams gave out, right where a sore area needed relief. He hoped it was enough to give his foot space to heal. Until then, he'd have to favor his left foot.

Outside, the sky lit up with streaks of deep purples and magenta. The streaks evolved slowly, changing shape and color. At one point a brilliant coral-pink took over the rest of the sky, only to recede again into the rainbow.

Ohj watched the sky recede to its original ocean-blue. He'd better get used to the idea of cleaning up a park. It wasn't such a bad thought—if boring. Hopefully someone would throw down a little trash now and then. He could ask the court to let him take care of this little park outside his courthouse. Might do him good to rest a while.

Swans swam in from different directions, heading for a foamy spot offshore. They glowed along with the brilliant sky, making Ohj wish for a pair of sunglasses. Bare flesh flashed to his right: pink, bronze, and silver, gold. The Botticellis were getting ready for a swim.

Even Ohj had to watch. Not in the mood to squat on the ground in his hole, he dropped down on a bench. He heard rustling as someone crept up from behind. Without thinking, he jerked around, as if expecting to find a demon.

A guardian took the seat beside him. "Aren't they just beautiful?" She offered Ohj an almond from a burlap bag.

He shook his head and eased back in his seat to wait for his heart beat to stop pounding in his ears.

The Botticellis stripped down to skivvies, fashioned from the same filmy material as the clothes they wore over them. The little Pomeranian danced around, hopping on the librarian's calves until she picked her up. The group didn't stand exposed on the shore for long. First one, then the rest, they all waded their rolling thighs and dimpled buttocks into the water. Swans bobbed around them, like ice cubes in a punch bowl.

The guardian held out the almonds to Ohj again. He shifted his gaze to the side not only to discourage conversation but also scout around the park for Vincent.

The dog yapped as the Botticellis splashed and jumped, their flesh jiggling, the water roiling. The swans were bounced around in the waves, forced to flap their wings to recover. Then, on cue, the group began to swim across the lake. They glided effortlessly, pulling themselves through the water as the dog paddled fiercely to keep up, too busy to bark. The ensemble was followed by the swantourage, appearing smaller the farther away they went—making the group easier for Ohj to look at.

"What a relief. Maybe they'll lead the swans so far out they won't find their way back," Ohj said, reaching for an almond.

"Don't worry, we can always send out a boat." The guardian's smile showed off two deep dimples. She took his hand and poured out a palm full of almonds, then bounced up, leaving behind a cloud of lavender in her place.

He considered the almonds in his hand, then leaned back. When he had responsibility for the park, he would ban boats.

A squirrel ran up the bench and over his scalp. A sharp, little claw barely missed one of his eyes. Ohj jerked up just before he was attacked by another one. The two squirrels chased each other around a tree then started back at Ohj. He threw the rest of his almonds at them. They rushed to pounce on the bouncing nuts, and headed back to the tree, cheeks full.

Ohj leaned back again and stared at the sun. As it warmed his cheeks, he concentrated. Eyes closed, he felt a growing warmth at his side. He focused on it, willing it to spread. He'd been injured far worse before: terrible gashes and gaping wounds that he simply ignored until they went away. He just had to ignore this too.

Instead of growing, the warmth on his side grew prickly, as if he were getting stung by bees. Next the patch began to itch. Another failed spot. Gloom threatened his optimism. When he went to rub the spot back to life, his fingers hit fur. A rough tongue caressed his hand. Vibration replaced the stinging when the cat began purring. Ohj got up, sending the tabby rolling onto its back. It stretched its legs straight out, then curled up again into a ball, content with or without him.

With a snort, he started to leave, but stopped. There were worse things in the park than a warm ball of fur. He looked at the tabby, now stretching out to take over his seat as well as its own. He sat back down, close to animal, and sighed.

Across the lawn, Vincent sat alone on a bench. Ohj scooped up the cat and headed in that direction. A different guardian aimed for the same spot right next to Vincent, so Ohj walked faster to claim the seat. Without slowing, he grabbed another cat along the way. Despite his effort at speed, the guardian outpaced him, reaching the bench first. Before she had a chance to sit, Vincent threw his legs up onto the seat and reclined back, folding his hands behind his head. The guardian stood a minute, then looked around for another place.

Ohj was starting to like Vincent more and more. Holding a cat in each hand, he kicked Vincent's legs off the bench with his foot. Vincent watched with one open eye as Ohj positioned a cat on either side of him. As both felines settled down with a yawn, Ohj gave Vincent a warning shake of his head.

"That's cool," Vincent said, watching the three cozy down. "We're still good, right? No problem with the Ronald-thing? You aren't going to sic a cat on me, are you?"

"You're safe." Ohj looked at the guardians on the grass, blocking his view of the water. A few had made a daisy ring around a person. They ran around in their circle, creating a blur of pastel. "No assignment yet?"

127

"No. And I don't know how much more of this I can take."

Ohj considered his companion, who sat in complete comfort on his cushiony bench: surrounded by beauty, a climate created to heal even the most damaged soul. It was the lack of contentment, combined with unbridled anger and resentment that reminded Ohj of himself. "You should witness. I think you're built for it."

"Nah, I prefer the trenches," Vincent said.

Ohj snorted. "And by trenches, you mean, Chuck E. Cheese?"

The cat had started kneading his thigh with little claws again. He unhooked each claw, one at a time.

Vincent started laughing. "Hey—are you forgetting my last assignment? My job is harder than it seems, obviously."

"Yeah, babysitting can be a...." Ohj stopped. Right at the shoreline, at the far end of the park, the High Witness looked over the benches. Once the witness found Ohj, he moved, crossing the grass in long strides.

Ohj forgot to breathe.

It's all over.

Chapter Seven

A guardian passed between him and the High Witness, momentarily breaking his view.

"All right, I can't stand it anymore," Vincent said. "What's the deal with the cats?"

Ohj did a fast comparison of how his own perceptions intensified when he walked through his window. Inside the window, not even memories were safe from him. He had no clue of this being's power. Were the capabilities of a High Witness even stronger? And he wasn't sure if, for the sake of professional courtesy, his own thoughts and memories were protected. He should have addressed all these small details before he took the job—asked a couple more questions. A little late now.

"Wow this must be a sensitive subject," Vincent continued. "If you don't want to talk about it, that's fine."

Ohj turned stiffly. "What?"

"The cats. What's up with the cats?"

Ohj had forgotten about the animals, doing their best to warm his legs. The real answer: he needed their body heat. But when he answered Vincent, he looked directly at the High Witness. "They are defenseless creatures. I would be a monster not to protect them."

"Wow," Vincent replied. "Whatever."

He needed a distraction. Oblivious, Vincent's eyes were screwed shut, his face now to the sun. Not that Ohj wanted to involve an innocent bystander. But where was Red when he needed him?

Ohj tried to clear his mind, and at the same time, appear nonchalant—as nonchalant as possible while hugging two strays. He forced his thoughts off his job. When his hand touched his pants, he tried not to remember how loosely they now fit, or of the awful pallor of his skin. A person ran past; so he tried not to think of the foot that throbbed inside his shoe. He looked around the park for help from the noise between his ears, but finally gave up.

He stared at the Witness and thought hard, *let's end this right now: come and get me.*

The Witness didn't move in.

A person in pink tights and toe shoes danced a few feet away. After a beautifully executed pirouette, she took a graceful bow at no one in particular.

Changing his strategy, Ohj clapped loudly. "Encore!" he shouted. "More." The ballerina started her dance again, making her way to their bench for a private show in giant, cascading leaps. Her white lace and tulle tutu bounced along with each jump.

A group lay idle on the grass, so Ohj waved them over. "Everyone dance!"

They got to their feet and began clapping around the dancer.

"What are you doing?" Vincent rumbled.

Ohj shouted to a small crowd a dozen yard away. "You got to see this."

The crowd hustled over, completely blocking Ohj from the High Witness. Someone brought a flute, another a guitar. They started with a slow beat, but soon picked up the pace, playing faster for the dancers. Vincent grimaced at the party, moving his feet under the bench so they wouldn't get stomped on.

Ohj got up and slapped him on the shoulder. "This will help your time pass."

Vincent commented under his breath as one cat scooted over to sit close to him.

Half way up the grass, Ohj heard hear a distinct, shrill whistle. One he knew a lion also heard.

His cleaning man gave him a thumbs-up as they passed in the hallway. Ohj signed, pausing at his door before going in to find out why. He went into his room and closed the door behind him.

The window droned, making him wonder if it ever shut off anymore. He'd begun to hate his job. His body was rejecting him. What terrified him the most was his growing hatred for the criminals he witnessed for. A new compulsion to slaughter every one of them, burned inside his heart. Any mercy he showed them wasn't from compassion, but self-preservation. Did the High Witness hear those thoughts?

He ran his hand over his head to clear his hair from his eyes. Several long strands clung to his fingers. He shook them on the floor and ran his fingers through again, this time using pressure. More hair came loose; enough to ball into a clump between his

131

palms. He dropped the clump on the floor with the other strands. He didn't have the energy to worry about going bald.

Ready or not, the view in the window cleared immediately.

Outside a gas station and quickie mart, gang members in an old Buick argued over the perfect time to start their robbery.

"You shoulda gone. Now someone's comin'," the driver yelled at his friend in the passenger seat.

A middle-aged man in a Hyundai pulled up to the pump behind them. The door clipped shut after the driver got out, card in hand. He headed for a pay station between the pumps.

"Man, just get this started," a teenager, neck inked with tattoos, yelled from the back seat. "He's nobody."

The driver went to pump his gas.

"Fuck." The teenager hit the seat in front of him hard enough to make the occupant jump. "You're such a vagina. Are you gonna do this, or not? Shit— you're wastin' our time, man."

Hector got out of the car and jerked his hood up over his ears. He eyeballed the Hyundai driver, who was busy fumbling with the gas cap. With one hand on the 9mm half buried in his sweatshirt pocket, he skulked across the concrete, to the quickie mart doors. After he pushed open the doors, he took one more glance around to make sure no cops were around.

Before the doors swung shut, he pulled his gun out and pointed it at the cashier. "Don't be stupid. Just get the money."

The cashier gave a sharp inhale. "OK. I got it. Be cool."

Demons packed the aisles. Hector shifted from foot to foot, waiting for the stash. He had a powerful gun—a 9mm. At close range, her death should be a fast one, if he aimed well.

Good, Ohj thought, because he had to let this one go. He kept his breathing even, his attention on Hector.

The clerk whimpered as she dropped two stacks of twenties on the floor, scattering the money all around her.

"You fuckin' with me? Seriously, bitch?" Hector checked the Hyundai's progress at the pump. The small car with its small gas tank, was still drinking in the fuel.

Demons surrounded. One, his bottom lip gone along with a chunk of his jawbone, elbowed Hector from behind while smiling at Ohj.

Ohj took his eyes off Hector for a moment. These demons stood a little straighter. Half dared to hold eye contact through the window, their once beautiful eyes burning with rage. They hated Ohj even more than they hated the humans. Ohj couldn't guess what drove these beings to such malice. Judging by their looks, whatever bait that had lured them away from paradise, didn't seem to be paying off. Now diseased and filthy, they attempted to cause as much damage as possible, one person at a time. Did they realize they were useless gnats, easily ignored? Or was this pathetic group convinced their efforts would win the entire war?

Two 6th grade boys, one the clerk's son, hid in the candy aisle. The boy watched his mother in the round mirror mounted on the ceiling. He was as angry as much as he was scared. He pulled a stick out of his pocket. One end was ground down to a point, freshly sharpened against the concrete outside the store. The tip still needed work to be sharp enough to scratch, but it was the only thing he had for a weapon, other than a Snickers bar. The boy figured if he ran with all his strength, the stick might do some damage. Especially if he aimed for the robber's heart.

After putting a hand up to quiet his friend, he started inching up the aisle. At the edge, he leaned forward a breath, just enough to see the robber around the corner.

Hector cocked his gun. His legs vibrated in constant motion. He wiped his mouth off on his sleeve.

One demon hissed at him. "Shit—she's messin' with you. You look like a fool." The demon wore a gown, possibly once white, but now gray with a tattered hem. Blonde, matted hair hung to her waist, and crusted wisps half-covered her face. Her eyes and cheeks were gaunt, and her nails had been torn out, leaving her nothing to scratch at Hector with when she raked her fingertips down his cheek. "You're gonna get your ass kicked for this. Want their respect? Take her out now. Clean."

Outside, Hector's friends raised their hands up at him. The Hyundai went for his receipt.

"What the fuck you doin' down there, bitch? Get me the godamn money," Hector got up on his toes and pointed the gun downwards at the clerk on the floor. He planned on blowing her brains out the second she came up, just for pissing him off.

"She's gonna screw it up for you." The female remained close to Hector. "Even that big bastard knows what I'm sayin'." She turned to Ohj. "Don't you? Tell him the truth; he's gonna get his balls shot off for screwing this up." She smiled wide, showing Ohj her black tongue. "Are you gonna help him, too? You gonna rush in and rescue him when his homeys tie him to a chair and shoot off his balls? First the right, then the left?"

The demons started to laugh. Two got behind the display with the clerk. One knocked over a carton of cigarettes, then grinned when Hector jumped. Ohj frowned. With Art's trial barely cold, it was too soon for another accident with a gun.

The Hyundai's receipt jammed. The driver hit the machine, resubmitted his numbers, and then headed for the store. The Hyundai's guardian walked beside him, relaxed—until he saw Ohj. With a jump in his step, he started talking fast to the driver. The oblivious man kept walking towards the quickie mart doors, with the guardian in his ear. The guardian ran to get in front of him and pushed with both hands. The driver stopped, turned around, and looked at the pay station again. At that moment, his receipt sputtered out. He swiveled around and went for the paper.

The clerk's son counted in his head to drum up courage. Ohj knew the boy's resolve to keep his mother safe was all the courage he needed. But his bravado would get his friend killed too. Ohj took another look at the friend. Trembling, pressed against the shelves, was Garrett—the boy from Wayne's kitchen table. Urine soaked his pants.

"Not again. How is this possible?" Ohj whispered, as the clerk's son kept mentally counting..., five, six, seven....

Observing Ohj's interest in the boys, demons crawled over to them. One touched the stick in the boy's hand. "Go for his eye. You're strong enough. And this stick's perfect."

A demon stood over Garrett. After the fiend got Ohj's attention, it bent down and bit the boy. Garrett twitched. He brushed at the bite, then rubbed. Another demon joined in, kicking the boy's stomach. Garrett wrapped both arms around his middle.

"You're dead. You are so dead. And it's gonna hurt bad this time," the demon told him. "Yeah, you know how this goes. Know all about it, don't ya, Sweets?"

When Ohj stepped in, the demons didn't budge. "What's this badass doin' here?" One laughed at Ohj. "Uh Oh. We're all in trouble now."

Garrett's pain rose up to greet him. Ohj felt the boy's horror: getting abducted, watching the dog tortured—knowing he was next. Again, the boy expected to die this afternoon.

Another car pulled up for gas. The gangbangers gestured wildly from behind their windows at Hector.

"Hurry. Before the cops get here," a demon yelled at Hector. "They're leaving your ass behind."

Ignoring the taunts, Ohj reached out and knocked the gun out of Hector's grip. It skidded across the floor, gliding to a stop under a magazine display.

The clerk's son hesitated, then slumped to the floor.

No death today.

Ohj got directly in the gangbanger's face. "Go."

"What the fuck?" Hector looked around his feet for his gun, then back at the cash register. He squinted at the Buick outside, and bounced on his heel, getting ready to run. "Shit."

Ohj also took a step to leave.

"Hey!" The clerk finally popped back up, but without the money. She had her own gun. She shot at Hector, hitting him in the chest. He teetered back, his hand on the spot where the blood soaked his shirt. Before Ohj had time to respond, the clerk shot again, knocking Hector backwards into a chips rack. Too late to save him.

The demons' shrieks exploded in the room, drowning out the boy's shout to his mother.

Ohj stared at the clerk, her gun still aimed at Hector as if defying him to rise and take another bullet.

"Now shoot the kids," A laughing demon yelled out.

Ohj had missed the fact that she had a gun. Preoccupied first with demons, second with Garrett, he'd completely overlooked this extremely important detail.

He stayed on his spot a fraction too long. The demons surrounded him. One demon got between him and his window. It was missing its leg from the shin down. Pus dripped down, making a small puddle where it stood. Its collar bones stuck out sharply, and its arms were no bigger than a child's, yet it challenged Ohj with a nasty sneer. "What are you gonna do now?"

"Before, or after, I take off your head?" Ohj grabbed the fiend by the dirty, satin shirt. He raised up the creature until its good leg dangled midair along with its stump. The demon flailed out, scratching at Ohj's right arm. With his loose hand, Ohj gripped its neck. The bones crumbled easily under the pressure of his fingers, as if he squeezed a dried corn husk. The demon's head dropped to the side. After Ohj let go, it fell like a pile of rags.

None of the other demons intervened or showed any grief that one of their own was gone. Humans forgotten, Ohj waited for another demon to challenge him. One or two backed up, but the majority stood ground, their hate aimed at him in a tidal wave.

By the time he got back to his room, the guardians had arrived. The demons ran, quickly losing interest in the scene. The guardians watched Ohj reenter his window. He could only hope that none saw the fight. At least he was certain that none saw him hit the gun out of Hector's hand.

Garrett's guardian walked up to Ohj's window. For a moment, Ohj thought he was going to follow him through. Ohj silently dared him, still hot from the confrontation. He lifted an eyebrow and extended a hand to assist the guardian inside. Catching the expression of two other nearby angels, he dropped his hand. Instead he gave the guardian a half-smile. The guardian didn't as much as blink as the window dimmed between them.

Ohj swiveled his chair, side to side, to let his temper cool. One full turn faced him at the door to the hallway: it was ajar. The book he'd propped against the door lay on the floor. He bounded out of his seat to look out. No one was within view; the hallway was quiet. He closed the door behind him firmly, leaning his shoulder into it with all his strength. This time he grabbed a stack of eight books to push in front of the door. The top book he leaned precariously into the door, ready to fall at the slightest movement.

He wrote up his account as he saw it—self-defense, and next began a new book for the clerk, in case he ever needed to hold her accountable. Pretty fearless with the gun, not to mention steady-handed, even emotionless. Hopefully, self-defense was all she planned with that skillset. Every few words, he glanced over his shoulder at the door. It remained closed, keeping the wobbling stack intact.

Absently touching his arm where the demon scratched at him, he looked down. Right above the elbow, the spot didn't hurt—just a small abrasion under the tear in his shirt. Pathetic that this was the best fight the demon had in it. With all the threats and bravado, they should have more ammunition at their disposal. Not to mention that its neck had splintered easily enough. They were as fragile as ever. He looked at his sword in the corner. Hadn't touched the weapon in decades. He used to keep the blade so sharp he could slice through two necks at once. Faster than just breaking them. He picked it up, admiring its weight. The sword was half his size in length, with a thick strap that secured it to his back. So, he wouldn't forget the blade, he carried it over to the window.

When he dipped his hands into the water, an unfamiliar, odor floated up. A clear goop filled the bowl. He looked down at his hands; they looked distorted, chalky underneath the surface. He scooped out a handful and let the fluid drip through his fingers. He smelled the back of his hand and recoiled.

It smelled like a dentist's office freshly washed with vinegar. Was hoping for some soothing herbs. This concoction smelled like it could to numb a tooth for a root canal. How could he purify with this? The gunk would glue all impurities to him permanently.

In those few seconds, the liquid had already dried, leaving behind a thin, enigmatic layer. He inspected his hand more thoughtfully, then smeared a little over his forearm. It glazed the skin with a whitish powder. He spread some over the other arm. It didn't sting, which was a plus. He patted more of the goo on his chest and legs, finishing with a handful wiped over his face.

The extra coating from the salve might just be the skin-cover he needed. Especially if it absorbed sun—then he would be in great shape. He hoped it would eventually dry clear. If he looked too odd, he could always wash it off in the lake. Might chase off the swans. That alone was worth the experiment.

With a layer of salve, his clothes clung to his skin even more. The thicker, still sticky areas bled right through, staining the shirt. Ohj looked down at wet ovals. The entire front of his pants was glued to his thighs. He yanked the shirt off, breaking the suction of the ointment, and tossed it over his chair on top of the red T-shirt. He was a wreck. For a moment, he wished he liked massages.

As he walked down the street, one guardian started to approach with a smile, but turned away at the last minute.

In court, the guards dragged Hector forward. Ohj held his thin book between both hands. The defending guardian stepped up to stand next to Hector. He wore a blue-and-grey flannel shirt half tucked in. His hair dangled in a short pony tail. A leather braid was tied around the wrist of the hand he kept in his jeans' pocket. He leaned casually on one foot.

Red regarded Ohj's slender book.

Ohj gave a wave to the defense. "I got nothin'...."

Hector's guardian began his testimony. "Hector suffered a lot of poverty and neglect." The guardian stood up straight, giving up his casual pose. "He had to join the gang just to...."

Ohj quit listening. He studied a relief on the wall closest to him: Moses throwing his staff down before Pharaoh. The detail was amazing, even without the color. Every individual whisker in Moses' beard was clear, as well as deep wrinkles from the responsibility of safeguarding a nation of people. The staff, in the process of turning into a very lifelike snake, slithered toward Pharaoh's feet. Ohj wished he had a staff-snake right then to throw at Hector's guardian's feet.

Red turned to Ohj. "Did another massive group of demons follow the boy?" Red asked.

Ohj shook his head, no. He was beginning to suspect the demons were following him, not the humans.

Red continued, "Doesn't seem like I need to come down too hard. The boy was pulled into gang-life out of self-preservation. That same self-preserving instinct convinced him he had to rob a store."

"Exactly!" The guardian said.

"Ok, he can go."

"Thank you, your honor." The guardian helped Hector off the floor as the guards unlocked his chains. He pulled Hector into a bear hug, rocking him back and forth. Before he let go, he kissed the human on both cheeks. "You're going to have so much fun here!"

Red hollered to Ohj before he could get out the door, "You're on a pretty good losing streak these days."

"No big deal." He could care less—more concerned about losing a foot. He wasn't sure but thought that gangrene might be setting in on the right.

"Next time, could you put on a shirt? Have a little respect." Red looked down to close the book on his podium, dismissing Ohj along with the rest of the court.

Ohj made it as far as the last step before he had to sit down.

He caught sight of Red's yellow robe, sweeping the ground as he turned toward the path that wound around the lake. The Judge moved further away with every step. Good. Ohj got ready to move in the opposite direction, until he caught sight of Red's companion. It was Asia.

He lunged forward to catch up, sprinting down the grass. As he closed the ground between them on the trail, it dawned on him that he had no plan. Did he intend to start a conversation? Make witty small talk? He slowed, and followed quietly, just close enough to grab hold of the healing wave that radiated from her. When he lagged too far, the sensation dimmed. So, he stepped up, keeping a steady pace, to stay just inside the circle of comfort. To anyone watching, he was part of their group.

She had a rich laugh, and her voice seemed softer than he remembered. Everything about her was warm, soothing. This was heaven. Unlike any other guardian he'd met. First, he tried to figure out how she did it. Eventually, he just closed his eyes, and let his feet find their way by following the sound of her voice.

"What's that awful smell?" Red stopped and turned.

When Ohj bumped into him, Red put up his hand to hold him off. "Ah, what a creepy surprise. You weren't about to mug us, were you?"

If Ohj had healthy skin, he might have blushed.

Asia smiled. He could only stare hard at her face, hoping her features would explain what exactly made her so unique.

"We meet again, my friend." She held out her hand to him.

He took her offered hand. Electricity zinged through his body. He didn't want to let it go, but his tongue refused to produce an excuse to prolong the contact.

"Might as well walk with us." She still held his hand, giving him the chance to pull away first.

"Hey, why don't you first run back for your shirt. We'll wait here for you," Red suggested. "Honestly, I'm not sure if you're contagious."

Ohj let her hand go.

"He's fine," Asia said. "Only needs better light."

While they walked, Ohj leaned in like a hairless runt. Staying tight to her side, he willed the walk to last a lifetime. Red rambled about the latest events of the City.

"Charming as country life here is, I have to admit I miss the City. And you," she turned to Ohj. "You need to go for a long stay. You'll find that the sun is much stronger there. It completely restores you. Whatever ailments you have will just disappear."

"I've been telling him that for ages," Red agreed.

Ohj managed a nod. "I lived there once."

He knew if he could go with her, his problems would dissolve. The combination effect would heal him. She wouldn't have to talk to him. He could quietly follow, two steps behind her. He looked at the hand she had touched: the skin seemed to shimmer a bit. To make sure it wasn't his imagination, he held it against the other. It did glow. After that small infusion of hope, he could stand up straighter. "When are you going back?"

"Soon, I think," she said. "But why are you still here? The country doesn't seem like a good fit for you. You strike me as the type who likes a lot more excitement."

Red joined in. "That's for sure. Ohj is better cut out for cliff diving with no chute, not hanging around a park. I can see him jumping straight onto rocks, preferably filled with vipers and broken glass." Asia's smile goaded him on. "Lying at the bottom, picking shards out of his hide until his bones are healed enough to walk. Then climb back up to the top to do it all over again."

"I've never tried that, but you're painting an inviting picture," Ohj said, only to keep the conversation going.

Regardless, she started to step away. "Hopefully, I'll see you both again soon. Maybe in the

City?" She left the two to finish the walk without her. Ohj stood watching as she walked away.

Red interrupted the spell. "We could use a little warning next time. Maybe some heavy breathing to let us know you're behind?"

Ohj checked out his arm. Scattered new sparkles twinkled up at him. He searched for more.

Red watched him. "You look like death. You started smoking, didn't you?"

A long canoe of guardians glided past them on the lake. They called out and waved for attention from the judge. Red waved back. "So, what did you want to talk to me about? You aren't in any trouble, are you?"

Ohj's gaze flew up from his bare chest. "What? Have you heard...?" He stopped his question short.

"What's so important that you had to hunt me down while I'm having a lovely walk?" Red asked.

Ohj looked closely at his old, and possibly only friend. Red was a judge first. Would he hold back high-level information from him? Of course, he would. But would he give him plenty of advance warning if things started going bad? A friend could only hope—but not expect.

Red turned away first. "Come on, I have to get back."

"Red." Ohj called out to him, stopping him from getting away. "Would you tell me if you knew anything bad about me?"

"Like you smell?"

"Like....."

"Like? Ohj, if you did something stupid, you have to let me know. I can't help you if I don't know what you did."

"I need more time."

Another group of guardians and people shouted out to Red as they paddled by.

Red nodded. "Then you are stupid. Sadly, you're my friend, which makes me an idiot." He walked on. "You know where to find me when you're ready to talk."

The sky began darkening. Ohj sighed, realizing that he'd just passed up the perfect opportunity to give his confession. He slowed down, trying to form the words in his mind. This wasn't going to be easy. He let out a breath and scratched his neck, then picked up his pace to catch up with the judge.

The same time he reached the benches, the sky went black: like a switch turned off, sending the countryside into complete darkness. Bodiless voices and murmurs filled the park.

Someone bumped into his side, another felt their way around him, palm over palm on the bare skin of his shoulders and back. Ohj swung out to push them away, but his hands sliced through air. Hearing somebody come at him from the opposite direction, he turned sharply, ready to block any touch. Again, his hands came back empty.

Too much contact.

Laughter rushed him from all angles. In the darkness, it sounded maniacal, getting louder with every dark second. If he ran, he'd likely hit more people: blind, and cackling, as they grabbed at him. Suddenly, he wanted his shirt. He crouched down to his feet, to wait for the moment to pass.

A light finally flashed, illuminating the park and giving Ohj a quick glimpse of the judge. He was stopped on the courthouse steps, looking up. Another glowing ball blazed across, sailing from one end of the sky to the other. A tail of fluorescent green followed, growing longer as it stretched out. Oohs and ahhs from the crowd accompanied the display. Three more flashes exploded overhead, each dragging green tails behind. After another two, the sky began pulsating in fluorescent rows. Now the ground could be seen, lit up with the light show. The sky came alive, breathing in waves of color. Streaks boiled though the air, undulating and snaking in and out of each other. The crowd cheered.

Ohj walked rapidly, swerving around one spectator after another. He followed every spot that lit up in front of him, determined to get to Red.

Before he reached the court, he sensed someone behind him. He kept walking, listening. At first the footsteps matched his own: same speed, step for step. Instead of going up after Red, he passed the courthouse, testing the footsteps behind him. When he stopped, the steps gained speed. Just as a witness came up fast, Ohj turned and braced himself. The witness brushed past, eyes on the ground, trying to find his way in the night.

As he caught his breath, another witness strode around him. It seemed to him that only witnesses understood that work still had to get done, no matter how beautiful the sky. Because of the shadows, he couldn't discern their expressions, read their mood. And better yet, they couldn't detect his either.

Someone grabbed his arm. Ohj turned, ready to attack.

Vincent stood right behind him. "Ohj, I think something's up." He looked around them in the darkness, then whispered; "First, they stalled by not giving me a new assignment. Now I'm not allowed in the City. It's no secret I'm going nuts here."

Vincent unknowingly gripped Ohj right on top of the demon's scratch. Ohj undid the guardian's fingers. "So, what? I know this place might seem like prison. Just because you're not a fan of the country, doesn't mean they're punishing you by making you stay."

"It's just that, after the whole Ronald-mess, I can't help but wonder if they blame me."

"Blame you? Why?" Ohj shook his head. "You're getting paranoid."

"It's crazy, right? But if something changes and they come at me, you'll support me? They won't touch me if you've got my back. Plus, you're friends with that judge. He talks to you. Will you check on things for me—make sure nothing weird is going on?"

Ohj blinked, hearing Vincent echo his own worries back at him.

"Everything is fine." His words were half-hearted at best, unable to even convince himself. "After they let Ronald go with all the damage he did? I'm surprised they didn't throw you a party for saving him." The last sentiment he could say with more certainty.

"Yeah, sure. Sorry. I must sound nuts." When a flash of light lit up Vincent, he was unsmiling, his brow furrowed. "So, where're you going now?"

"I'm going to work. No, you can't come with me. And, between the two of us, you might want to stay out of the witness pools."

After the outline of Vincent's shoulders sagged, Ohj softened his tone. "Alright, there's no law saying you have to use your own pools. And as far as leaving the countryside—try to be patient. They're probably looking for the perfect match for your next person, just to make it up to you for giving you Ronald. I'm sure you won't have to hang out here much longer."

"Maybe you're right. Thanks." He left slowly, watching his feet.

When Ohj got to work, he didn't rush inside but stood on the path. Passing figures behind used the light overhead for guidance, moving around him, instead of bouncing off. Shadows lingered in the crevices, filling in the landscape and deep sections between the trees.

When a guardian came close to touching him, he stepped closer to a hedge of bushes. The dark inside the greenery appeared to grow more solid, take shape before his eyes, and he sensed movement. Inside the rustling, he listened for whispers, vulgar murmurs. He took a step closer to the liquid black and leaned forward. Unconvinced that a shadow so dark could be only air, he reached in his hand. His fingers met with branches and leaves. Before standing up, he looked around him, then backed up the path to keep the hedge in his sight.

The dawn of light started; crimson rows spreading out to push away the shadows. Once alone in his room, he peered at the one light on his ceiling. His pupils constricted into tiny dots. The brightness hurt his eyes, as much as it frustrated him. For the first time, he scanned the walls for a switch to turn the thing off. Finding no mechanism to control it, he picked up his chair and shattered the oblong light source. Shards rained on him and the room darkened:

except for the window, which now maintained a constant glow.

He put the chair back in front of the desk and leaned over to pick up the shirts that had fallen. His arm ached as he used the shirts to dust glass out of his hair and he could smell the salve on his skin. Images of surgery wards and battlefields flew through his mind. The thought of adding another coat was unbearable.

Thinking he caught a piece of flying glass, he lifted his elbow for a better look. The demon's scratch burned an angry purple. So much for the ointment. He tore out a sheet from a clean book and wrote down the words, "Bring back the mint," then put the note in the antechamber beside the bowl. The bowl was already freshened with a new batch of clear goop. He picked up the bowl and set it outside the door on the ground, along with the note. He was better off unclean.

He rubbed his arm before putting his shirt on. His sword still leaned where he left it. He picked it up and put it on. The weapon felt good. The strap fit neatly across his chest, with the sword resting straight up between his shoulder blades—easily reached by either hand. He reveled in its familiarity; the weight of it felt like an embrace. The window started buzzing loudly, getting brighter; lighting up the room more than any overhead bulb or chandelier could hope to.

He faced an alley, squeezed between windowless, brick buildings. Three men leaned in over a fourth. The fourth shrank away from them, as if trying to dissolve into the brick wall. Filthy clothes with extra layers, all of which were at least two sizes too big. Though oily bangs fell over his eyes, the peach fuzz gave the boy's age away.

"It can't be." Ohj massaged his temples. Garrett—again. Just hours before, Ohj had left him inside a gas station. A few years apparently passed for the boy. Those years hadn't been kind. "What now?"

The men threatening him had access to a home and a shower. They were clean and well groomed, wearing new jeans and expensive sports shoes. One had a two-hundred-dollar, green track suit on—Allen. Allen connected the dealers to the buyers. Garrett wasn't clean enough to deal. He worked as a look-out of sorts, a messenger boy.

Demons lined up. Ohj scanned the alley quickly, counting a dozen and a half. They were large, quiet—without the usual buzz and taunting. Some leaned casually against the wall, one with a foot behind to prop him up. Others had their arms crossed, as if waiting for a bus. Instead of harassing the humans, every one of them faced the window; and looked straight through it at Ohj.

Ohj turned back to Garrett. A thick gold ring weighed down the finger Allen pointed in Garrett's face. One of the other thugs threw a punch into Garrett's stomach. Garrett bent over in pain. The demons didn't cheer the fight on. They didn't bother poking at the kids, or whisper to them. They just watched Ohj. Humans walked past the alley without bothering to look inside, let alone intercede. Alley fights and bad drug deals were just too common to get excited about.

This fight was already unfair, with three adults against one kid. The can of gasoline one of the thugs held, made the odds worse.

The thug in the fur-lined hoodie, unscrewed the cap from the gas can.

Chapter Eight

Allen pulled Garrett up to face him. "Look, loser, I'm payin' you. Said I'd be back to mess with you if you fucked up."

Garrett's eyes swung back and forth, between Allen and the gas can. "Hey man, I did what you told me. I stayed here all night. They didn't show up."

The furry hoodie began shaking out the fuel from the can. Gas splashed Garrett's face and shirts, as well as hitting the other thug, the wall behind them, and the trash at their feet.

"What the fuck you doin'?" The other thug spit and wiped his face with his sleeve. "Watch it, dumbshit."

"Suck me." Furry hoodie tossed out one more bonus splash.

Ohj shook his head. He didn't have this in mind for Garrett when he saved him from Wayne's table. Or the quickie mart. Destitute? Facing *another* violent death? How much did one person have to take in their lifetime? He stepped into the alley and stood between Garrett and the hoodlums. To this boy, mistreatment at Allen's hands felt normal. That angered Ohj even more.

One demon straightened up. As he walked towards the humans, it wasn't a limp that slowed him down. His gait was lazy, as if he was already bored with the scene. Ohj didn't turn his head until the demon stood across from him. When he did, he had to look up to meet the demon's eyes. This creature was a warrior. His skin had the same dull appearance of a death-mask, loose and grey like the other demons. And he smelled like a centuries-old corpse, but his arms and legs were intact, and he still had both eyes in their sockets.

"What do you make of him?" the demon asked Ohj, from over Garrett's head. His eyes were hard, black, and there was no warmth in his faint smile. "Thought you had everything figured out, didn't you? But he doesn't quite fit—this boy."

Two others joined him, both just as tall. One with a sword at his hip. The other held a spiked club, which rocked slightly from the movement. An oozing gash ran down the side of his face, but the arm that gripped the club looked strong enough to deliver a solid blow.

"You're helping us more than you know." The warrior demon put his hands in his pockets and stretched his back until it cracked. "Makes me wonder whose side you're on. Not sure if you even know."

"Why don't you explain it to me," Ohj said. "I'd love to hear your take." He kicked the gas can out of the one thug's hands. It splashed all three hoodlums again, tipping over as it flew a couple feet away.

"Hey, bitch," the thug yelled. "These are new shoes." He shoved his cohort hard.

"Fuck you, bitch. I don't give a shit." The other one pushed him back.

Allen ignored them both. He reached into his pocket for his cigarettes and lighter.

Garrett wiped his stinging eyes. "I'm sorry, man. I swear I didn't fall asleep."

The demon's focus stayed on Ohj. He wore street clothes—not the dirty rags that seemed to be the required demonic uniform. This meant he either stayed out of trouble, or he was strong enough to fight all his battles without soiling himself.

"Are you ready to talk?" he asked Ohj.

"You have some secret information?" Ohj returned. "Some great wisdom to bestow on me?"

"Actually, I do: first, you're not supposed to keep saving this kid," the demon said. "That one's free, but only because it's so obvious."

Ohj shrugged. "You're right—that's obvious. I never am supposed to save them. But I know who is." He turned away from the demon and the four humans with one step, then shouted out for Garrett's guardian. The alley trembled as if hit with a small quake. "I can't keep doing your work for you. You need to get here and do your job."

Allen put a cigarette to his lips.

"Come on, bro, give me another chance," Garrett begged Allen. He reached into his pocket and pulled out a few crumpled dollars and some change. He offered the handful to Allen.

Allen laughed. "You kidding me? What am I supposed to do with that?"

The demon continued, talking over the humans. "Second, we aren't the ones who want him dead. You think we're the bad guys? We're not. Stop fighting us and you'll see." He shrugged. "You might even find that you prefer us. With us, you can protect this one, and any other human you want. Finally live like you were created to. It's a good life."

Allen touched his cigarette to the flame, inhaling until the end glowed red. Then he reached out to Garrett.

"Hey, I can do better...." Garrett started.

Allen held the lighter to Garrett's face. But just as the flame popped up, Ohj bumped his arm at the elbow, bringing the lighter back towards his chest. The flame hit Allen's synthetic sweatshirt and connected with flecks of splattered gasoline. Before Allen dropped the lighter, his track suit had caught fire.

The cohorts stared as Allen yelled, "What the fuck?"

"Shit." One took off down the alley. The other followed after a second glance at Allen.

Allen jumped around, trying to beat out the flames on his jacket. Garrett leaned against the wall, frozen.

Ohj felt a hand on his shoulder. He turned, at the same time, reaching back for his sword. Garrett's guardian stood in the alley, wearing the same gray hoodie and jeans he always wore.

The demons receded to the street.

Ohj stepped into the guardian's face. "What have you been doing all these years? What happened to him?"

The guardian straightened his posture. "I've been with him all along."

"I can name three times, including this one, where you seemed to be out on a break." Ohj shoved him back a step. The guardian took that same step forward. Ohj pushed him back again. "Aren't you supposed to be protecting him? You should have stopped him from following Wayne to his kitchen. And jumped between him and Hector's gun. But you were nowhere to be found. And the best part—now he's homeless, at the mercy of drug dealers?"

Allen started screaming when the flames caught his hair. He jumped around, slapping at his head.

"I usually follow these assholes throughout their lives ...," Ohj said, pointing at Allen. "This is the first time I've followed a victim."

"Why are you following Garrett? That's not your job." Although shorter, and smaller, the guardian didn't back down.

Ohj was glad he didn't. He punched a finger into his chest. "I'm doing my job. But you're throwing him to every wolf you can find. Like you're deliberately trying to destroy him."

"I can only do so much," the guardian shouted back. "My hands are tied and its torture. No, not torture—physically impossible. I don't get a window to hide behind. You think I'm a coward—fine. But I can't watch when he's about to get slaughtered. Because if I do, then I will stop it. There was nothing more I could do for him—he's marked." The guardian pointed at Garrett's leg.

Ohj had seen it. On the kitchen table, the odd-looking birthmark. He loosened his grip on the guardian.

"At first, I thought it meant he was blessed. This kid is anything but. Demons are all over him." The guardian pulled his sweatshirt away from Ohj's grasp. "All I know is that I have spent his entire life guiding, leading, protecting—anything, to help him avoid one tragedy after another. Nothing works."

A door in the alley opened. "What the hell's going on out here?" A man in a stained, cooking apron took a step out. He ran back inside, yelling, "Hey, there's a guy on fire in the alley!"

Garrett inched towards Allen, who was now slapping at the flames that spread to his legs. Garrett leaned in to help beat out the flames that dissolved Allen's clothes around his skin.

"*You* take a cursed boy and follow him though life. *You* feel his pain, day in and day out," the guardian shot back. "I'd like to see if you could do a better job, only without your security blanket."

Garrett screamed. Ohj and the guardian both turned to look. Garrett's shabby, gasoline-soaked clothes had caught Allen's fire. Now both boys were jumping.

Ohj sucked in his breath and Garrett's flames rose higher. He lunged to put out the fire that burned the boy, but the guardian moved first, getting in between them. The guardian held Ohj off, even as Garrett screamed for help. "Don't."

The flames grew the hottest around Garrett's head, burning off the bulk of the gasoline. Even if Ohj saved him, he'd be burnt beyond recognition. Ohj considered Garrett's options; destined to die in some burn ward or survive the hospital only to face something worse.

Hearing Garrett's heart beating faster and faster, Ohj moved around the guardian. He aimed two fingers right at the frantic muscle and struck fast. Garrett's heart stopped, and he dropped to the ground. The flames caught the splattered gasoline on the trash around his body.

The man in the apron jumped back out into the alley carrying an extinguisher. Another man, with a bucket of soapy dishwater, was right behind. A cab driver jumped out of his cab, yelling for help. He popped open his trunk and grabbed a blanket. As the dishwasher doused Garrett, the cook sprayed Allen from head to toe with the extinguisher.

Standing beside his guardian, Garrett watched the commotion from a safe few feet away.

"Is it over?" Garrett asked him.

"You're all done." The guardian put his arm around the boy. "Let's go home."

Ohj watched them leave. As the cabbie tossed his blanket over Garrett to finish off the rest of the flames, Ohj turned to his window.

It was gone.

He took a few steps back to look again from a different angle. Still he couldn't see his work room or even a shimmer from the window. He put his palms up in front of him, as if blind, patting at the air to check for any warmth, any heat. None. Hoping he simply miscalculated the window's position, he ran a few steps over, patting, searching the cold bricks for his window.

"Now, that's interesting," the demon warrior said into his ear.

Ohj jerked around. The alley had filled with even more creatures than before.

"But I could've told you that was going to happen." The demon smiled. Laughter from his cronies filled the alley, as the humans worked to save Allen's life.

One demon stepped on Garrett's body to get closer to Ohj. She held a dented and rusted cleaver in each hand, and her skirt was torn away to give her legs more space to move.

Ohj reached behind him and drew out his sword.

"It doesn't have to go like this," the warrior said.

The same two demons who stood with him before, held their weapons out in front of them.

"We both know it does," Ohj responded. He slashed out with his sword, separating one demon's arm from its shoulder. The arm fell to the ground, still holding the sword. Ohj sliced again, separating its head. The body dropped to the ground. Ohj turned on the being with the club. He shoved the tip of his sword into the demon's chest, then leaned in, using his weight to push the sword all the way through until it broke free of the skin at the back. Ohj braced his foot on the demon's hips and pulled, extracting the sword. The demon fell, joining the first.

"I knew you were a maniac," the warrior breathed, not bothering to look at the bodies at his feet. "But this, this really is insane. You have any idea how many of us there are?"

Ohj turned on the woman with the cleavers. She was still looking at the warrior, waiting for his signal when Ohj sliced off her head. The head rolled over to Allen. If the human picked that moment to die, he would get a very ugly welcome into the afterlife. He still breathed yet, his hands out in front of him, not much more than melted lumps and bone. A paramedic kneeled beside him to start an IV, unknowingly setting his bag in a puddle of the demon's blood.

"Suit yourself." The warrior signaled with a nod of his head, then stepped back to watch.

A shorter demon raced in with a banshee scream, swinging a blade over his head. Ohj caught him in the waist. He used both hands to carry the swing through, until the demon was cut in half. Another charged, taking his place, his only weapon being razor sharp claws. Ohj cut him down quickly, then raised his sword for the next one. They came at him one at a time. Once Ohj realized this, he paced himself, taking every advantage of the poor strategy.

After the first dozen, the warrior kicked one demon close to him in the seat of its pants. "Get in there. Now."

The demon charged in to join another, who had already taken a severe head blow. Before Ohj finished with those, the warrior sent in another two. Ohj sliced and swerved, turning and cutting, wave after wave. When he caught sight of the numbers waiting their turn to attack, he noted their lack of enthusiasm. They inched backward, shuffling from foot to foot, eyes on the warrior, as if hoping for a stand-down order. Since the stronger ran in first, the later demon-waves grew shabbier. By the time he got to the last three, the creatures just looked at him, then turned and ran. They left behind only the warrior, his mouth still curled in a slight smile.

"Eventually you'll want to talk," he said to Ohj. "It's just a matter of time. And I'm patient enough to...."

Ohj swung his sword.

The warrior raised his hand in front of his face just in time to catch the blade. The blade sliced through his hand, shearing off two fingers and part of his palm. The smile disappeared.

"That's going to cost you." The warrior turned away, leaving Ohj alone with the humans.

Ohj looked around at the carnage in the alley: human and spiritual. Allen was gone, already in some emergency room, and Garrett's body lay under a tarp. Two officers pressed the cook and the cabbie for details. Pedestrians crowded in at the entrance of the alley, suddenly interested, drinking up the tragedy as eagerly as the demons.

The alley was cold. The sky gray. Too many of the humans were heartless. Ohj rested the tip of his sword on the ground. He wouldn't survive long here in this hostile place; feeling the callousness of every human around, surrounded by constant evil. The smell alone would drive him mad.

A warmth grew beside him. He turned slowly, afraid to hope. The window waited for him. Ohj stepped through before it changed its mind.

A completely dark room met him on the other side. Trying to control his breathing, he held his sword out in front of him, waving it slowly, back and forth to fight off any attack. As his eyes adjusted, he could see bits of the broken glass on the floor. He relaxed the sword, remembering his outburst with the overhead light. As he reached behind to sheath his sword, he saw movement.

On the wall directly ahead, where he knew the door to the antechamber to be, there was a shift. The wall appeared to ripple, like the undulation when a stone hits water. He blinked twice, then squinted, willing the effect to repeat itself. Instead, the wall became solid, as if the ripple never took place.

Smelling of gasoline and burning flesh, he stepped carefully, bringing his bloodied sword with him into the antechamber. There was no water: no bowl at all on the table.

He opened the door and looked down at his feet, hoping at least to find the discarded goop. The bowl was gone, along with the note. Soon he would have fresh water to bathe with, but nothing to help him now. He unstrapped his bloodied sword and let it slide to floor. His arm throbbed. He didn't remember getting hit. Reaching up to rub the spot, he felt a dampness on the fabric. Not one weapon caught him; he was sure of that. A stain spread out from the old scratch. He pulled off his shirt to get a closer look. Infection had set in. The line was flaming and puckered. Pus trickled out from a few breaks in the skin. The odor rushed up at him.

He used his shirt to wipe off the pus. Before dropping it on the ground he wiped the blood off his sword. After stripping off the rest of his clothes, he grudgingly pulled on the fresh set that waited for him on the chair.

As he walked the long hallway to the bathing pools, he took deep breaths, hyperventilating on the clean air. Five other witnesses, three females and two males, soaked in separate pools. He would have to pick one of those to share. The female on the end floated in the middle of the most promising one—the smallest. If he climbed in with her, his privacy was guaranteed. He undressed slowly, hoping she would get out by the time he finished.

After he pulled off his shirt, he looked around for a reaction. No one seemed to notice the wound. He turned that arm away as he finished; undoing his pants and letting them drop slowly down his calves. The door opened. A witness, already undressed under a robe, strode in. He threw the robe off and grabbed a private corner in one of the longer baths. Ohj kicked off the first pant leg. The female stretched out, touching the opposite end with her toes, discouraging anyone from squeezing in across from her. Ohj stepped out of the other pant leg.

Once he neared the pool, he moved fast, stepping into the water and claiming a small end for himself. Still feeling exposed, he dipped his head under the water. His pool mate made no sound when she got out, leaving Ohj to discover himself alone when he came up for air. Ohj waded to the middle and stretched out. Floating on his back, he looked up at the skylight that allowed visible rays to hit every pool. He angled himself directly under one ray, letting it caress his head and shoulders. He wiped at his skin discreetly, desperate to clean himself of all the contamination. As he scrubbed his arm, removing any leftover discharge, he looked around to see if anyone noticed. No one complained outwardly, but three more witnesses left, including the newcomer. As Ohj let the water rinse away all the death, the last two witnesses stepped out of the pools.

At peace, he closed his eyes. Until he remembered the rippling wall inside his room.

The water sloshed over the edge when he sat up straight. He knew what it was—a window. It happened so quickly; he might have missed it if it weren't right ahead of him. If he hadn't broken the light, he probably wouldn't have noticed it in the first place. The question was, was it always there?

He didn't know anything anymore; he was just an underling doing his job. A shiver danced along his skin and goose bumps popped up on his exposed arms and shoulders. He dipped down to his chin, better repositioning himself under the light again.

But he wasn't doing his job.

So, why didn't anyone stop him? Or come haul him off? If what he was doing was so wrong, why was he allowed to keep doing it?

It obviously wasn't his dirty secret anymore, if ever; windows were everywhere. He let his legs float to the surface as he rested on his back. Not only was he rescuing desperate people, but now he was also killing demons. Was he on double duty? Maybe that's why no one stopped him: because he was an asset? Quiet. Discreet. Doing a job no one wanted or dared to do. He started propelling himself with his hands, going forward, then backward again, in the tight confines of the pool.

When he climbed out, he glanced back at the pool. The water was dark, and the bottom obscured: like a stagnant pond. The other pools still sparkled with floating flower petals. He dressed and got out of the room.

He absently massaged his arm as he walked to the courthouse. He couldn't put off telling Red any longer—but he'd long passed the time for counsel. Time only for confession and judgement.

A shadow crossed in front of him. He looked up and met the eyes of the Viking. He held Ohj's gaze, unflinching. Ohj nodded at him as they moved past one another. Shots of adrenaline traveled to his chest. Another witness came towards him. Ohj kept his eyes forward but couldn't help a quick side-glance in her direction. This witness too stared right at him. The eye contact was direct, locking onto Ohj's, pulling his head in her direction as they passed. He picked up his pace.

With the courthouse steps in view, he started running.

There was shouting from the park. The usual park-drama. Ohj started up the steps, not bothering to look.

"I said, Halt!" the command was firm, and loud.

Ohj froze, then turned slowly, keeping his hands down.

A skirmish made its way towards the courthouse steps. Somehow, the command wasn't for him. He deflated with relief.

Three uniformed soldiers wrestled with a guardian. Another arrest. This wasn't Ohj's problem, so he started to turn. But when he saw a flash of white-blonde, curly hair, he took a step closer, wanting to make sure he was wrong.

Though Vincent fought the soldiers ferociously, he only succeeded in knocking loose one of their hats. One soldier got control of the flailing by crushing Vincent's blonde head under his arm in a solid head lock. Vincent still tried to run through, pushing the soldier along with him a couple inches.

Another soldier threw all his weight on Vincent's back, driving him to the ground.

"Hey!" Ohj ran at the soldiers full force, knocking one off his feet.

The captain held his hand up to slow Ohj down. "This doesn't concern you."

The third soldier still had Vincent on the ground, with a knee in his back. He ignored the interruption as he began winding chains around the guardian's wrists.

"Hold it," Ohj yelled. "What's this about?"

There were three soldiers against the two of them—two, if Ohj could get Vincent out from under the one soldier. These were easy odds. He looked around the crowd for another witness. There might not be loyalty amongst witnesses, but they did share the love of a good fight. He saw the female witness in boots and waved her over. She picked up on the opportunity and pushed her way through the crowd of guardians. Two more witnesses joined her, until four large witnesses stood up against the soldiers. Vincent stayed on the ground, chained.

"All right," the captain said. "We aren't letting him go, no matter what you want, but I'll give you a few minutes to state your complaint, so you'll get out of our way. Make it brief."

"First, he's not a criminal," Ohj started. "Take off the chains."

"He's not a criminal?" the captain exclaimed. "What? Then there *has* been a huge mistake, because I've got orders to drag him off to someplace really bad. And I need the chains, because he'd rather not go."

"Not if we can help it," the female witness grumbled.

Ohj looked down at Vincent, face shoved in the grass.

"Is this guy a friend of yours?" the captain asked quietly. He dipped his head to get in Ohj's line of vision.

The eye contact made Ohj ease back. He motioned to the crowd. "Aren't we all friends here? I just want to know the charges, and why the mistreatment. I don't think that's too much to ask." He looked to either side of him at his witnesses, who nodded in agreement.

"We'd all like to know," a witness said.

"Alright, what do I care?" The captain shrugged. "Consorting with the devil—that's the charge."

"OK." The witness in boots turned and walked off before taking a breath. The two others were already ahead of her.

Immediately alone, Ohj laughed. "And what's *that* supposed to mean? Cuz I don't appreciate the insult."

The soldiers looked at each other. "Wow, don't flatter yourself," one said. "You witnesses sure put yourselves on high pedestals. You're not that important."

Ohj stared at him, trying to comprehend.

The captain squinted up at the sky. "Let me simplify for you as best as I can: your *friend* was found consorting, as in dealing in a friendly manner, with The Devil. Not some ugly witness, but the real- life, as in, you're-going-to-hell-now, devil. No kidding. But you probably already knew that, didn't you? Being close and all."

Ohj raised his hands in the air and took a quick step back.

After the soldiers finished chaining up Vincent, they yanked him to his feet. The crowd made way as the three kept a tight circle around their detainee.

Ohj stayed with them, if only because they all walked in the same direction—the courthouse. He still needed to talk to Red. Now even more.

Vincent didn't make it easy on the soldiers. He let his knees and feet scrape behind him on the steps, toes down to create as much drag as possible. Eventually all three soldiers grabbed him up by his waistband and carried him the rest of the way.

Ohj followed shamefully. He silently wished the guardian would stand up on his own and face the court with some self-respect.

The last soldier hesitated at the top of the steps, blocking Ohj from following them inside. "You aren't still looking for a fight, are you?"

"No. I have business with the judge— unrelated, but official business."

The soldier closed the doors after letting him in. "Join the party, then."

Ohj glared at him but stayed quiet.

Red left his podium, meeting the soldiers half way as they dragged Vincent up the aisle. He called over the soldiers' heads. "Ohj, I'm glad you're here. We might need your help."

The soldiers kept wary eyes on him.

"There won't be a trial for this one, your Honor," the captain said to Red. "He's already been found Guilty Without Recourse. We're here to escort him to the gates."

Ohj looked at Red. "What is this? No trial?"

Red shook his head at him. "Don't get on the wrong side of this fight. He's had all the trial he's going to get. Now help them take Vincent to the gates."

Ohj's jaw came unhinged.

"Yeah, grab a leg," a soldier said. "He's a kicker."

Vincent came alive. "No. You don't understand!" he screamed. "Take me to the Throne. I have to get to the Almighty. This is a mistake!" He starting jerking, rocking the soldiers that held him.

Red motioned to Ohj. "Get in there."

Mouth still slack, only Ohj's eyes moved to Vincent.

"He's his friend—he's not going to help us," a soldier said. "If anything, he has a part in this."

"Nonsense," Red snapped at the soldier. "Ohj, you have to trust me on this. He isn't who you think he is. This wasn't his first encounter. He's been warned before."

Ohj walked over numbly. He took hold of one of Vincent's legs to stop it from kicking out the teeth of the nearest soldier. The soldiers and Ohj each held an extremity, with Vincent face-up, toward the sky.

"Ohj, what are you doing?" Vincent screamed. "Help me. Don't let them take me!"

Submissive, Ohj walked with the three soldiers as Vincent started bucking, throwing him and the soldiers into each other. "Help," Vincent screamed upward. "Please, let me explain! I didn't do anything!"

Ohj stopped walking and looked up at the cloudless blue overhead. Pulled to a stop, the soldiers turned back to him. Ohj held tight, watching the sky to see if Vincent got a last-minute reprieve. He hoped with all his heart that the reprieve came, because he wasn't sure if he could help carry his friend to the gates of hell.

"Please," Ohj whispered. "Let this be a mix-up."

It started snowing. White flakes drifted down on top of them through the open roof. A cool breeze cut through the air, as delicate crystals came to rest on top on Vincent. The soldiers' hats were dusted white and Vincent's shirt began to blur from the powder. Ohj looked at Red; unsure if this was the reprieve he hoped for.

Red held out a hand and let a few flakes fall onto his palm, then shook his head—no. The sentence was good. He motioned for them to continue.

Vincent started bucking and screaming again. Ohj wanted to drop the leg and demand more answers but didn't dare. If there was snow, there might also be lightning. They continued through the inner courtroom and turned right, to the long, dark hallway where Ohj had never ventured before. At the end of this hallway, he could see twenty-feet-high, double-wide doors waiting for them. Vincent must have felt that he was getting closer. With the strength of ten guardians, he started pulling his arms and legs away from his captors, slowing them. Each step became more difficult.

"You cold-hearted bastards!" His face turned bright red. "You're turning on one of your own!"

When they approached, the doors swung inward automatically. A wave of dammed-up stench hit them face on. Ohj had to let go of Vincent's leg with one hand to cover his mouth. Icy air shot through

171

him. They walked several more yards before Ohj could see their goal; gates made of four-inch-thick wrought iron. The blackened metal was a chaotic pattern of intertwining people. Horrible gaps were cut into the design in intervals, in case anyone wanted a peek-a-boo view of the abyss beyond.

"God, no!" Vincent screamed louder with every step closer.

Above the wrought iron lurked a blackness that Ohj tried not to stare into. He didn't want to see into the shifting depths. He felt the cold, smelled the flesh of whatever scurried around. He didn't want to see the source. Those gates opened outward, swinging silently. A noisy wind flung small bits of matter at them. Vincent kept trying to buck them off, contracting his torso like a frenzied inchworm trying to escape a crow. Ohj's infected arm began to ache more from the strain, so he switched, awkwardly gripping the pant leg in his left hand. He then pulled his shirt over his mouth and nose, so he could use both hands again. He walked with his chin tucked in to keep his lips covered. The rotting smell was so strong he could taste it.

"I'll come after all of you," Vincent screamed, before turning wild eyes on Ohj. "You'll be here with me. I will eat you alive. You think you're safe? You'll be here next, with me cutting out your heart. I'll gut you myself, you whore's son."

Ohj was sorry he came.

The soldiers seemed fearless, with the two in front marching them all in, deeper and deeper. If he were in the mood, he would laugh at how just minutes before, he'd challenged these soldiers to a fight. These beings—who could walk into hell so easily.

They continued, past the gates. Their feet found their way on the dark ground, hitting rocks and kicking at scattered bits and pieces. No telling what had settled under their feet, but he was sure they weren't traveling over seashells. A cold whistling in his ear sent chills down to his arms. From all corners of his eyes, scampering and bustling scratched for his attention. Despite the movement, he kept his gaze forward, waiting for the signal to let Vincent go.

Ohj thought that they had trudged in far enough, but the soldiers kept marching forward to some unknown target. He suddenly pictured getting his sleeve caught in the chains during the ruckus. Then getting left behind with Vincent as the soldiers ran for safety. His arm began to shake, and he pursed his lips to slow his breathing.

Then, an even more horrible thought dawned on him: what if they were transporting him too? What if this was a trick? And here he was, conveniently walking himself past the gates, to his own damnation. What was he thinking, admitting to being friends with a damned guardian? Like the one soldier said, that made him guilty too. He wasn't great friends with Vincent, had barely met him, yet he'd just defended him as if they were long lost brothers. A brother would not only be aware of demonic connections; likely he would be involved.

For the first time in his existence, he wanted to run in fear. His knees started to buckle, and he almost lost his grip.

Vincent remained frenzied, his voice getting hoarse. "Ohj, you're going to get jumped by the biggest mother fuckers you've ever seen. We'll be waiting for you, lining up to shred you to pieces."

173

At the risk of falling, Ohj kicked Vincent in the back. "Shut up!" His words echoed horribly and he instantly regretted them.

Red's voice behind him made him jump. Ohj hadn't realized that he followed—assumed he stayed in the comfort of the courtroom. "That's far enough. Put him down."

They had reached a thick pole, four feet tall, with a fat metal ring sticking out the side. Some sort of hitching post. It leaned precariously from a millennium of people trying to pull themselves free. This offered another explanation for Vincent's chains—to chain him to the post. That's how they were going to keep him from following them back to the courtroom like an abandoned dog. Whatever monster showed up with the key to unchain him, Ohj wasn't going to stick around to see. He got ready to run. Even if he had to trample Red to do it, he planned on being the first person through the nasty gates.

The three soldiers put Vincent's extremities down carefully, while Ohj dropped his leg as if it were brimstone. The captain began to chain Vincent to the post.

Vincent's voice went guttural. "I was there the whole time, you sanctimonious prick!" He lunged for Ohj, but the chains kept him back. "I loved every second as Ronald gave those whores what they deserved." He started laughing hoarsely. "I wasn't avoiding some human tragedy by staying out of sight, you fucking idiot. I was avoiding *you*."

When Ohj turned to run, Red no longer stood behind him. He had free access to the path. He kept his eyes on the wrought iron gates, willing them to stay open long enough to let him through. Half way there, his foot slipped on a sharp clump. When his hand went down into the shadows to regain balance, it touched something wet and matted. He snapped his hand back and balled it into a fist. Behind him he could hear Vincent shrieking, "Don't leave me. Ohj, we had a deal!"

Chapter Nine

Those words gave Ohj all the motivation he needed to run even faster. The wind whipped something wet into his face. Just two feet from the gates, he didn't bother wiping it off. The steel scrolls seemed to quiver in anticipation; ready to slam shut on him. He dug down, grit his teeth, and flew, landing on his stomach. Still walking ahead in the white hallway, Red turned and looked at him.

But Ohj wasn't home yet—he still had to make it through the double doors. Crawling wasn't going to get him there fast enough. He got up on his feet and started running again. He could still hear Vincent calling his name. Even after the wrought iron gates clanged shut behind the guards, he could still hear Vincent howling out to him.

Ohj bolted past Red and made his way for the doors. He was first one in. To his credit, he didn't lock the doors behind him. Instead, he kept running, not slowing until he got to the inner courtroom. Then he threw himself down again on his face, arms stretched out over his head. A few flakes of un-melted snow remained on the ground. The snow seemed like an eternity ago. He closed his eyes and saw gray, twisted carcasses hobbled in the shadows. The smell of vomit and death remained as fresh in his nostrils as the sweet breeze that filled the courtroom.

"Are you okay?" Red bent down on his haunches at Ohj's head.

"I didn't think I'd make it out. I thought I was going to rot in hell," Ohj whispered.

"Ohj, that wasn't hell." Red patted him on the head. "You have to get up. I have court."

The soldiers didn't hide their smiles as they stepped over him to make their way outside.

"Hey, if you're interested, there's a search and rescue job opening up," one called out, over his shoulder. "All you have to do is go in there to look for people."

Another one added, "But you have to last more than five seconds if you're actually going to find anyone." The soldiers all laughed.

Ohj got up. In the bright, snow-dusted courtroom, he too could see the humor. Here was big, strong Ohj, running from hairballs and smelly mist. When he walked out into the sunshine and looked down the court steps at the beauty of the lush, green park, he could still almost see the humor.

Relief over his freedom brought an epiphany— the High Witness wasn't investigating him. All those times, he was probably keeping an eye on Vincent. Just a terrible coincidence. The very worst time for Ohj to draw attention to himself, and he had to start hanging out with a fallen angel.

He walked down the steps slowly, smiling for once at the free spirits who used to annoy him. He looked around at the beauty: the velvety flowers, shockingly white swans, the shiny flecks in the granite steps. Two enormous statues stood at the bottom of the steps. He'd never paid any attention to them before. Marble, polished as smooth as glass, gave them a silkiness that begged to be touched. Somehow, he'd walk by them thousands of times and not even look, let alone touch. He inspected one closely—an angel offered a hand to a child: Mercy. He looked over at the other one. It too depicted an angel; only this one turned its back, while stepping on a monstrous, yet desperate, creature: Un-mercy. Ohj looked away.

He was tired. He wanted to go to bed for a thousand years. But first he had to wash the crud off his hands: in water, in mint, in goop—he didn't care. The sun burned hot, doing its best to revive his spirits. He felt it on his head, heating his hair and scalp. He felt it on the back of his neck, as he watched the ground pass under his feet. He kept his hands balled into fists, lest he try to rub the tired out of his eyes. Wrestling with Vincent, jarred his sore arm. He didn't need to look at his shirt to see the fresh stain, he could smell it. He dragged himself to work, going straight into his antechamber, just to dip his hands in the bowl.

His minty water was back. How did he think he could live without it? He scoured his hands, then cupped them together to splash the water on his face. He breathed in deeply; missing the cool freshness. Then he washed off all the crud that hell had spit on him. He couldn't stop. Naked, he continued to wash off damnation, rat bones, and whatever else he'd carried out with him. The mint stung, setting his skin and infected arm on fire, but he didn't care. It felt good. Clean.

He dressed in the new, fresh clothes, and went to sit at his desk, planning on resting a while before walking home. He squinted up at the bright light in the middle of the room. Not only did they fix it, it seemed they also upped the wattage. The window hummed, radiant and pulsing. He didn't care. No matter how much the window begged.

He quit: it was official. He was now done with death.

Later he might be cleaning up after swans, but now he needed rest. He put his head down and closed his eyes. Images flashed in front of his lids: cold images of gloom and beasts. It had been dark wherever they dropped off Vincent, obscure shadows of terror. His imagination made up for the lack of light, filling in all the corners with beings, tortured into deformity.

He heard voices inside the room with him. Two women haggled in Arabic over the price of a pomegranate. They sounded as if they stood right behind him. He lifted his head to look. The window ran at full speed—with no one standing in front of it. A man's voice, raspy from years of smoking, bested the women's haggling, shouting out the miraculous benefits of the fruit—justification for such a high price. Another man joined in with an assessment of saffron.

Ohj put his head back down on his arms and closed his eyes again.

Chickens clucked behind him. Children shouted, and a new argument began over the freshness of a skewer of lamb. The window heated his back comfortably, enticing him to get closer. If he stood in front of it, he could also warm his front. Or maybe he could lean into it and let the layer of warmth envelope him, while he slung between the two worlds as if on a hammock.

He pushed back his chair and walked over.

The market was crowded, dusty, and the burning sun threatened the freshness of the produce. Several awnings lined up, shading the tables covered with vegetables, fruit, and spices. At the far end, vendors displayed baskets and rugs, as well as cheap jewelry and knock-off art. A few vendors cooked lamb on large spits, swatting flies in between shaving off meat. They delivered the spicy shavings in a pita topped with cool yogurt. Despite the heat, the vendors wore long kurta shirts over their pants. Head to toe in fabric, the women kept an occasional eye on their offspring as they worked. Not a rich market—no gold or silver. But it was a full one, busy with people shopping for that night's dinner.

Ohj put his hands up against his window to warm them. He stood close to it to let it heat his thighs and stomach.

A small group of children chased an escaped chicken. One lurched for the tail, knocking over a barrel of small onions. The stand's owner yelled at the kids, waving his arms over his head. With his next breath, he aimed his rant at the man working the stand next to him: the chicken's owner. This man's booming voice stopped the children mid-step. They then hustled back to the dirt, to each gather the most onions.

For a moment, Ohj forgot why he was there. He watched the scene through half-shut eyes, swaying a bit against the membrane that separated him from the humanity. A tall, American couple walked around, heads swiveling and wide-eyed. The woman squeezed her purse tight against her ribs as she looked around for a small souvenir. Even if she did find the perfect knickknack, she wasn't sure if she could let go of her purse long enough to pull out the money. Likewise, her husband kept his eyes open for pickpockets, suspecting every man and child.

Three local women sat on wooden crates, drinking tea, and whispering about one's new husband. The new bride relished in the fact that she could finally join in wifely talk; even if it was to admit the marriage bed was less than thrilling.

And Ohj saw guardians: dozens of them, walking, following, and glancing around. One stopped an old man from a fall that would have broken a hip. Another simply followed a preteen around as he searched for one girl he'd talked to the day before. The guardians appeared so relaxed in their natural state. Ohj leaned back on his heels and watched.

Then his eyes strayed to the horizon. At the foot of the hill, a mile outside of town, a solid line of demons stood ground. Thousands. All waiting. Held at bay by the large number of shimmering angels.

The guardians noticed Ohj first, then next the demonic army. Nervousness permeated the air when they realized that something was wrong. They began to shift, move more quickly. They started talking in people's ears, trying to impress on them a sense of urgency—to walk, run, as far away from Ohj as possible. One guardian pushed a man forward, causing the man to trip. Instead of hurrying along, as the guardian hoped, the man stopped and turned to look at the ground behind him.

The Americans were easy to infect with apprehension. Although the woman had just found the perfect item, a hand-woven scarf, it took only a couple words from her guardian to get her moving. She hung onto her purse with both hands as they made their way to their hotel. Three guardians stood next to the vegetable stand while the children fought over the last few onions that had rolled under the table. One guardian put his hand on the owner's shoulder. There was less urgency on this spot directly in front of Ohj. The guardian scrutinized the distant multitude, then looked grimly back at Ohj.

When Yusuf walked up stiffly, sweating under the weight of a heavy jacket, the vegetable vendor wasn't nudged or inspired to run—only calmed by his guardian's hand.

Yusuf, a Jihad recruit at thirteen, had just turned twenty. He'd been trained as a cook, but his new position held much more responsibility. Explosives were stacked on his chest, held in place inside a canvas vest. A head scarf covered an extra roll of explosives near his neck. Added at the last minute, it was first in line for detonation.

His steps were slightly staggered, and he breathed through his mouth, despite his burning throat and tongue. He unknowingly kicked a stray onion. It rolled a few feet towards the children. They screamed and jumped for it. Yusuf flinched at the children's sudden commotion. He stood, blinking at the scene. The wayward chicken took that moment to bob over and peck at the dirt near his feet. Its appearance set off a new round of shrieks. The children now aimed for the chicken. The chatting women looked up, frowning at the noise.

Surrounded by young children, this was Yusuf's opportunity to change his course. He could turn and walk, very carefully, back to the car that had brought him. Maybe even plan another attack at a different time. Time froze, though only for Yusuf and the guardians. Motionless, each waited for the decision.

As more guardians cleared out of the scene, the demons inched forward. Ohj leaned down and picked up his sword. He kept his eyes on the demonic army as he pulled the strap over his head.

Yusuf closed his eyes. Sweat soaked his clothes as if he burned with a fever. He wanted to scratch at the weight at his neck. Careful not to jar any wires tucked inside his jacket, he reached into his pocket for the remote. He began chanting under his breath, summoning courage.

Decision made.

Guardians went on the move. One kicked a ball. A few children chased after it, away from Yusuf. Just as they got close, the ball sailed off again, another thirty feet. The children screamed with laughter and ran. Demons swarmed in closer.

Ohj left the window's band of warmth. He didn't stop until he breathed in Yusuf's face. The young man lifted his head and opened his eyes towards heaven, praying for a good outcome—that many people die. He also prayed that he finds his way quickly to his reward in martyrdom. All around, guardians and demons watched. They stood in quiet rows, all facing Ohj. People milled around, some wandering dangerously close to Yusuf, unaided, as their guardians stood transfixed by the scene.

One of the women pointed out Yusuf. Her friend stood and screamed. The screams spread through the crowd and people began to stumble over each other to get away. One woman tripped on her long gown, pulling a man down with her. A mother ran to grab her child away from Yusuf's feet. Another mother, with a toddler in her arms, only understood that she should run. But not knowing why, she followed the first mother, straight at Yusuf.

Hand still in his pocket, Yusuf fumbled with the remote, lining his thumb up just right.

Ohj grabbed Yusuf by the shoulders and cupped a hand at his throat. He concentrated on the charge, wanting to block it from getting to the explosives. All he had to do was absorb the vibration, stop the connection—and no explosion. The mother running blindly bumped into Yusuf. Yusuf pushed the button. Ohj shoved the woman, tossing her into a vegetable stand.

A furious blast shot straight up like a fire cracker, seen from the four corners of the marketplace. Yusuf's head, eyes still open to heaven, hit a mark in the sky, paused, then cascaded back down to earth.

The headless body stood on the ground with Ohj's hands still on the shoulders. Ohj let go and stepped back. The body dropped, just as the head crashed through an awning. The head, black hair soaked with blood, rolled a few feet. The people all stopped running and stared. The guardians also stared. The market got quiet, except for the chicken, which walked over for a peck at Yusuf's rocking head.

The demonic legion charged forward. As they made room at the foothill, another swarm appeared, filling in the ranks at the back. The guardians began to corral in their wards, getting as many moving as possible.

Ohj drew his sword.

The strongest rushed in first. Just as in the alley, the front ranks were all warriors. Bigger than he, probably stronger. Hundreds of these fighters filled his vision, until he couldn't look far enough beyond them to find a single raggedy creature.

His infected arm shook from the weight of the sword, and his hand lost its grip on the hilt. He switched the sword to his left, and again held it in front of him, waiting for the first demon to get close enough to slice at. The window stayed warm on his back. He concentrated on the strength of the heat, fully aware that at any second it might go cold.

As if he were going to walk through it again anyway. He grinned at the thought of surviving a fight with this legion. Not even with two good arms. As he stood ready to challenge the horde, he felt every second his age. And even older.

The demons came to a stop within spitting range. They were fierce. Never prone in their other, heavenly life to wear tutus, or twist balloons into fun shapes. These were all serious fighters. Maybe witnesses. Their weapons were sharp, intended to cut Ohj into molecules. Several eager beasts climbed over the top of the crowd, stepping on others' heads to get a better chance at him. Even at a standstill, the crowd pulsated and churned like boiling oil.

The demon warrior from the alley walked up from the side. Ohj turned toward him, keeping his sword alert. The demon didn't stop, but kept walking, until the sharp tip of Ohj's sword pressed into his chest.

"I knew you'd be back," the warrior said. "Been expecting you."

Another demon walked up beside him. Ohj's sword dipped from the shock when he saw Vincent. Both his forearms were covered with deep, open gashes where the chains had been, as if he'd clawed himself loose. In the short time, his skin already lost its shine. His hair was now ashen, and the blue in his eyes gone. He no longer resembled a fresh-faced Kewpie doll, but a graveyard cast-off.

Ohj jerked the sword in his direction.

Vincent's hands shot up. He smiled broadly. "Whoa, I'm not here to fight. I'm here to witness. Don't worry; I won't interfere," he added. "And I will take great notes on every bit of your torture."

The warrior nudged Ohj's sword aside. "Relax. I'm still pissed, but I'm a reasonable man. I think you'll work out just fine here with us. Of course, you'll have to go through one helluva initiation ritual. You're not very popular right now. And we condone hazing. We're firm believers that pain is good for the soul." He came closer and put his hand on Ohj's shoulder. "Since we're to become friends, it's time we get on first name basis. I'm Elias."

His skin gaped between crude stitches where Ohj had sliced off two fingers. The cold mud that flowed through his veins seeped through the gaps onto Ohj's shirt.

Feeling wet ooze on his flesh, Ohj reached to push the hand away, but faltered when he saw their hands side by side. His own was just as gray, peeling, with the toughness of a cadaver. His muscles ached like never before, and winter was buried deep in his bones. Worse, the change in him had a life of its own: a momentum beyond his control. He already hated humans, at least the foul ones. Was never that crazy about guardians. When he looked at the demons, he was looking at himself.

He lifted his sword to Elias' chin. "I'd rather die."

The warrior laughed. "I don't think you understand. That's not one of your options."

Ohj took stock of the legion. Shaking with excitement, they cooed and salivated as they waited for him. Warning chills coursed through his body. There would be no noble, *fight to the death* for him. They weren't going to let him die. And as he lived, he would continue to evolve, his mind slipping further every day. Until he wanted to stay. Then he too would stand at the sidelines, cheering, as a rapist sliced up a child.

As images of his future unfolded, a terror took hold that he'd never experienced before. Three large demons took advantage of his shock. They rushed up on him and heaved him into their crowd.

Hundreds of hands grabbed, punched, prodded. Predatory faces blocked out all light as they leaned in, to spit and jeer. Every inch of his flesh was desecrated. He tasted decay as obscene fingers were shoved inside his mouth. More fingers were jammed in his ears, muting the shrieks around him. His eyes squeezed shut involuntarily against gouging nails.

The creatures holding him down on the ground next lifted him up. He felt his body rise. Hands propelled him along over the heads of the demons.

Traveling over the masses, he had an opportunity of fresh air. He filled his lungs with several breaths, clearing the fog. He realized he still held his sword; fingers frozen in a death-grip around the hilt. After struggling to lift the sword up, he sent it down on skulls. Over and over, he lifted and dropped the blade onto the crowd, blindly slashing away. Demons just below jumped out of the way of the sword, until the lopsided group sent him crashing to the dirt.

He used his bloody sword to push himself to his feet. Laughter surrounded him, with Vincent's loud howls above the rest.

Smiling broadly, Elias stepped up. "I can't tell you how much fun this is going to be. You're not here a half hour, and I'm already having the time of my life."

Ohj opened his hand and let the sword drop to his feet. Eyes closed, he threw himself back on his heels. Falling straight back, he hoped with all his heart the window would be there to catch him.

Warmth enveloped him, encasing his cold, bruised flesh like a warmed blanket. Shock intermingled with relief as the window welcomed him home.

Flat on the floor of his room, he stared ahead at the demons. They rushed up in a fury, gnashing their teeth, clawing at the air where he'd stood seconds before. As they pushed and shoved, a beast on top was thrown forward. She hit the window, then cascaded through, landing behind him in his workroom. Rolling in a ball, she screamed an agonizing wail. Ohj jumped up, covering his ears. He looked at his sword, still with the demons in the dirt. Instead of going back for it, he lunged at the demon, desperate to get her out of his room.

She tried to move away as he grabbed her with both hands. Before the window could close her in with him, he threw her with all the strength he had left. She landed on top of her cohorts and was absorbed into the herd.

Not even sure if the window closed, he tripped to his antechamber. Dirty clothes and towels still lay in a heap. Only dirty water at the very bottom of the bowl. He looked around, desperate. The shirt Red gave him still lay over the back of his chair. He pulled off the shredded remains of his shirt. The scratch was now a blackened, open gash. Dark streaks of the infection coursed down his arm. The smell was unbearable, and he could hardly lift it. Carefully, he pulled the red shirt over the bad arm, then over his head. *NO APPEALS, NO LAST MEALS* screamed out in bright white letters. This was the cleanest he was going to get.

Feeling the stares of every witness he passed, he kept his eyes straight ahead. The guardians hushed as he passed them. He didn't look to see if their expressions showed loathing or sympathy. Didn't care. He passed the courthouse and kept walking. Even Red's intercession couldn't help him anymore. He had to get his case to the Throne.

There were just a few buildings after the courthouse, then a row of scattered cottages. The road straightened out as he walked, before curling again into a forest of trees, with trunks big enough to drive a semi through. The birds chirped noisily, flapping their wings before taking off to test another branch. The rustling leaves soothed him, tempting him to stop and take a break inside the thickening. No one would see him. If only he could stop a minute and lean against the bark, let the trees calm his nerves. Crickets chirped, again encouraging him to take a seat on the cool moss that cushioned the ground between the tree roots.

Instead, he kept moving, however slowly, urged on to reach the City. Relieved as he'd been over his belief that the High Witness wasn't investigating him, he missed an important fact. Whether the High Witness followed or not didn't matter; Vincent certainly had him in his crosshairs. Vincent had targeted him before the interventions ever began, seeing some terrible potential that he himself didn't recognize. The High Witness managed to get a twofer.

A thin string of smoke curled up from the middle of a copse. He could smell the burning wood: the rich incense of pine cones and chopped timber. He left the path to take a quick look, his steps muffled by fallen needles. A clearing revealed a small, crudely built, log cabin. The chimney rose out from a roof of bark and peat. Fur pelts hung over a rail surrounding a wrap-around porch. Ohj walked in closer and a touched a stiff, black hide, curious if it was real.

He needed to sit down, so climbed the porch steps. At the top was a bench carved from one thick log: two growling bears with all eight paws flat on the ground. From the saw dust, Ohj guessed it was just recently finished. He sat, letting the bears ease the pressure of his burning legs. The seat was uncomfortably hard, obviously man-made. Still, he was so tired. And he felt chilled. He looked at the shade surrounding the cabin. The tall trees blocked too much of the sun to keep him warm. His hands were ice. He eyed the pelts.

The windows had thick drapes. Probably to ward off cold as well as eyes. The drapes shook. So, the owner was inside.

Ohj waved his hand over his head. "I'm not staying."

A thin voice came from inside the cabin. "Get along, then. Nothin' for you to see here."

Ohj pushed himself off the bear-bench and climbed down the porch. "Just so you know," he called out, behind him. "Pretty sure there's a strict, no-poaching law."

He made his way back to the forest, rubbing his hands together for warmth.

The pine trees eventually made way for bright maples. Yellow, orange, and vivid red leaves crowded the branches. Buckets strapped to a few of the trees collected sap for some forester's syrup, or glue. A few deer nibbled at the side of the road, not bothering to look up as he passed.

He was visibly shivering by the time he came to the end of the woodland. A road veered sharply to the right, curving along an enormous wheat field. Instead of following the road, he went straight into the wheat.

He marched a new path, leaving a trail of bent wheat. The wheat slowly straightened back into shape, closing him in from behind. The stalks had baked all day under the hot sun. They hugged his body like a blanket fresh from the dryer. All he could see was a buttery yellow: to the side, in the front, and behind. He smiled, completely in over his head. If he sat down no one would ever find him. Who would come out here? He could exist for a million years, buried in these tall, rustling stalks. Not even a hermit would want to live alone in a wheat field, so no chance of bumping into a poacher.

When he paused to enjoy the thought, his legs began to cramp, alerting him that if he stopped now he might not be able to get up again. He moved on, pulling one leg in front of the other. Half way through the field, he had to stop to get his bearings and catch his breath. When he finally cleared the silky wheat and stepped onto grass, he felt exposed. He stood, panting, at the edge of a cliff. The City was just on the other side of that cliff, nestled in the valley below. He sighed and reminded himself why he made the trip. His short walk to the edge was unenthusiastic. A breeze immediately picked at the warmth he'd gathered in the wheat field. He walked to the edge and looked down.

Panorama lay at his feet. Stunned by the sight, he finally let himself sit. Miles of gold covered the valley: a brilliant, endless pool set on fire by the sunlight. Skyscrapers stood out, reflecting the blue sky with their polished siding of crystal, pearl, and bronze. Houses were scattered; some huge, some just large, but all very small from Ohj's viewpoint at the top of the cliff. While Paths and tiny crystalline steams connected the homes, gleaming roads led up to outer gates made of luminous pearl and precious stones. The golden city sparkled with every color, floating in the valley like a heavenly mirage.

He let his feet dangle over the edge. Asia was right—the sun did seem to shine brighter. Had he never seen the City from this viewpoint before? Never took the time to stand in awe, or as he left, get the urge to turn and take one more look? Maybe he'd just forgotten, but he couldn't remember in all the ages living there, of truly appreciating its stunning beauty. He couldn't account for that fact. Except to guess that he'd been too spoiled by his diet of daily contentment.

Now, starved to death, he wanted to open a vein to draw it all in.

Giraffes loped outside the City walls, bending their heads to touch their noses to the ground. A couple of elephants made their way through a pasture. Hiding within that pasture grass, he knew, the lions would be sleeping.

Birds, a flock of thousands, dipped low just over his head. Row after row of synchronized geese headed toward the City. They flew first in one direction, and then crisscrossed, taking the sky with them on their way to the horizon. He watched the birds with longing. Truly free, they had no thoughts of death or pain. Just lived in weightless abandon.

All he had to do was start moving. Climb down. Straight below swung the pearly gates, the streets of gold, and even a tiger if he wanted to pet one.

But the City looked so far away, miles down and miles across from where he now rested. And he was so tired. His legs were leaden, and he could barely hold up his head.

He brushed wheat fragments off his arms, picking off a few yellow pieces that stuck to his damp skin. Despite how good it felt to rest, he knew he shouldn't waste any more time, but start heading down. To get himself up, he focused on that growing sense of urgency. When he looked straight down at the jagged rocks below his feet, he shook his head. He was going to be here a while.

He looked for an easier way down. If he went right, the clearing led back to a little winding path that dropped off gently into a pasture. Might take longer but seemed more manageable than the sheer cliff right below him. All he had to do was get up on his feet, and the rule of motion would get him to that path. If he could just get inside those gates, stand on that golden street, he would be OK.

He flexed his leg muscles to heave himself up. They refused to cooperate.

Clanging and footsteps came from behind. He would have to wait for them to pass anyway. No matter who it was, the last thing he wanted was company. Especially not all the way down the hill. He leaned back on his hands. The ground felt as soft as swans' down. He dug his nails in to scoop up some brown dirt flecked with gold.

"Ohj." The strong voice behind him made him blink. "You need to come with us."

He turned around at the waist. Nine soldiers stood on the grass. The soldiers towered over him, with healthy, shining skin and rippling muscles. They wore steel over everything: chest plates, helmets, arm bands, leggings, ankle guards. And swords. Drawn in front of them, ready to chop Ohj in half. He recognized the one in front—the captain who had dumped Vincent off. He'd exchanged his other team for an even bigger one.

Ohj started laughing. "Nine? You need nine to come get me? I'm flattered, guys."

None of them smiled.

"Get up. We have orders to detain you," the captain said. He pulled thick chains out from behind him. The chains could anchor a yacht. Each link was as thick as Ohj's wrist, the whole string long enough to wind around both his feet and hands, then loop around behind him once for good measure.

Ohj fell on his back, laughing harder. Here he was, barely able to stand. There was no way he could take on the weight of those chains. "Someone's going to have to carry me piggy back with those things on." He looked at their serious faces and sighed. "All right, let's get this show on the road. Come pick me up."

The soldiers looked at each other, then at their leader, waiting for an order.

"I'm glad you still have your sense of humor. You're going to need it. Now get up and come with us," the captain said. "I'd like to point out that there are no witnesses to jump in to help you, so you might want to come along easily. If not, we're more than willing to hogtie you and carry you in on a spit. Up to you."

Ohj used all the strength in his good arm to push himself to the point where his leg muscles could take over. He stood in front of the soldiers. The eight back-up soldiers all shifted, taking a defensive stance, their swords still out in front.

Ohj put his hands up. "Calm down. I'm not going to resist—I'm guilty. And you don't need the chains. I'll come without a fight. I've been expecting this. I did intervene. I lost my objectivity. The High Court has no choice but to fire me. So, I'm going to take my reassignment—preferably in the park outside Red's court."

The backup soldiers relaxed their swords. But the captain still held tight to the chains. He turned his head to the side, thoughtfully. "Intervening? First I've heard of that one. The more you talk, the more charges you add up for yourself. If I were you, I'd pipe down. I'm taking you into custody to face eight counts of murder."

The tingling began at Ohj's scalp and traveled down his spine. He searched his mind trying to remember all the deaths. There couldn't be eight. Besides, the lives he saved should count against the lives that were lost. Even still, there couldn't be a headcount of eight, unless the court blamed him for the suicides. At least two classified as suicides. Yusuf didn't expect to survive that bomb strapped to his throat. That's why that particular job was called a *suicide* mission. No one could pin that death on him.

Ohj's mind continued to race. What's the penalty for murder? Was it being forced into a job cleaning up after swans? He didn't think so. He looked over the group again, finally recognizing another one from Vincent's horrible ordeal. He was hiding in the back. They weren't going to detain him—they were going to drag him off to that hellhole. Those were chains to tether him to the hitching post.

Vincent and all those demons were going to get another chance at him after all. They were probably lining up, waiting for him that very minute.

Ohj pulled himself up to his full height.

"You didn't bring enough soldiers."

Chapter Ten

Ohj kicked out at one of the swords that rested at a soldier's foot. He caught the razor end of the blade and flipped it over to grab the handle. He kicked at another sword, grabbing it off the ground where it landed in front of him. Ohj now stood in front of the nine soldiers, holding two of their swords. If they noticed that he held one of the swords poorly, they didn't show it. The soldiers in the back passed their swords up to the front line. Ohj took a step towards the cliff's edge to gain more room to fight.

The captain showed no shock that the beaten-down witness came up fighting. "You only have two hands, unless those crazy feet of yours are going to manage the other seven swords."

Ohj looked behind him. He had just another foot. Maybe his best odds would be to jump and make a run for the City. If he could make it to the Throne

Room without getting stopped, at least he could plead his case.

"Even if you could fight off all of us, which in my opinion is extremely unlikely, where are you going to go?" the main soldier asked.

Ohj got ready to jump. He could throw one of the swords at their heads, to slow them down, but then he would have one less sword. He needed his two swords for show. Although, the real trick would be not to impale himself getting to the bottom of the cliff.

"How about this...," The captain took a step forward. "We let you have one-hour head start to wander around in the wheat again. If we catch you, you come with us without trying to chop off any of our arms. If we don't catch you, you go free."

Ohj put his sword to the soldier's neck to stop his advance. Another soldier jumped forward. Ohj held out his other sword to block him. "I have a better idea. You accompany me and my swords to the High Court in the City. There, I will give my defense. If I'm found guilty, you can take me to that pre-hell to get eternally damned. But if I'm shown mercy, I do whatever I want, which might be to still chop off your arms."

"There's that sense of humor again," the captain said. "Only problem is, you're not allowed in the City. My orders are to take you back to the country."

Ohj's hope sank. The High Court had already declared him an outcast. "Is that so wise: taking me back home? You'll have to get me past all my friends. There could be quite a mob scene."

"I doubt it." The captain shook the chains at him. "Now put these on."

"I walk on my own, without chains."

"All right, but hand over the swords," the captain said.

"I keep the swords too."

"What—are we stupid?" one of the back-up soldiers said. She looked at her leader with bulging eyes. "Who's bringing in whom?"

Ohj pushed the soldier back with his sword. "If we go to the courthouse, without the big hoopla, there will be less chance of one hundred witnesses jumping to my defense." It was a sad bluff. He'd be lucky if one took notice of his hoopla. And the one who did notice was guaranteed not to care.

The Captain dropped the chains. "You get one sword and you stay up front with me. We're taking you to the country court, but there will be another judge appointed—instead of your friend. You'll take whatever judgment you get, and then you will put these chains on yourself and face your outcome, no matter how terrible."

So, he was going to get a trial. Ohj handed over one of the swords, grateful to let his arm hang.

He turned behind him to claim that one long, last look that he'd never taken of the golden valley. At a soldier's nudging, he tore away from the beauty and joined the captain. The eight soldiers fell in behind. They took the trail around the wheat field and headed back towards the maple tree grove. Ohj stayed in front with his sword. He planned his defense as they marched through the forest, trying not to think that this might be his last time also seeing the beautiful trees.

They moved at a trot, with Ohj struggling to keep up. He worked to stabilize his breathing, while also keeping his feet clear of the sword. Even his good arm started to ache, and his legs were numb. He tripped twice and got trampled by the soldier jogging behind. He had to stay clear-minded. Break the cases down, one by one, just in case the court did hold him accountable for every death in his window. When bundled together, they looked like deliberate treason. He started reminding himself of each case, and why he made the decisions he did. If he described each one separately, every hurt child, every scared adult, maybe he could piece together the mercy he needed. He would have to approach his own trial like he did all the trials—with precise detail. He'd done it a million times. He could do it again. Only without notes.

As they walked past the hermit's cabin, Ohj tried not to think of the hitching post. Or the fate that went with it; so much worse than death. The soldiers remained silent as they cleared the forest and started up the road to the courthouse.

They slowed down when they got close. The captain drew his sword and scanned the area around them. Guardians filled the park as usual. When the soldiers marched up, the guardians all stopped to look. Ohj's breathing grew rough when he got close enough to see the courthouse doors.

Half dozen witnesses also loitered. They too stopped to stare. Ohj wished he weren't in the front, getting scorched by all the gazes. Witnesses walked toward the courthouse steps, coming in from different directions. Unsure whose side they were on, Ohj watched the large beings emerge from the park and pathways.

The soldiers stiffened, also unsure whose side the mob planned to take.

They all met at the courthouse steps. Ten witnesses stopped Ohj, the captain, and his soldiers from going any further. Others climbed up the stairs to block the entrance. Red came out of the courtroom and pushed his way down to the captain.

Red looked at Ohj's sword and smiled. "I'm going to defend you."

"I'm going to defend myself," Ohj said. "I can handle the trial just fine."

"We'll see." Red nodded at the mob of witnesses. "Let us through, please."

Ohj didn't look at the angel statue of un-mercy as he passed it on the steps. His legs started to tremble as he followed, his breaths compacted into short bursts.

Before they entered the doors, Red turned and called out to the mob, "Everyone is welcome to watch."

Ohj frowned at him. "My entrance was humiliating enough. I prefer to take my shame privately."

Red leaned closer. "You need all the support you can get."

They walked in—Red first, then Ohj, followed by the soldiers and the mob. Ohj looked to the side as they stepped towards the podium steps. Guardians had already taken seats. Halfway up, Asia sat. His heart lurched. He watched her as they passed. Red turned him forward to face the Judge.

His Judge already stood behind Red's podium. Never at High Court, Ohj didn't recognize the being. Piercing eyes, and white robe of breathing satin, the Judge looked down from a psychological dais much taller than the physical one he stood behind. He burned with an internal fire, light radiating out and around him. A beam shot straight to the back of Ohj's skull and he had look away. Fear filled his lungs. He found no mercy in the Judge's gaze. This Judge would see past his entire defense and instead stay focused on the crimes. Red walked him right up to the podium.

Ohj wasn't surprised to see his nemesis, the High Witness, standing in his old spot to the right. Ohj shook his head, losing yet another chunk of frail hope. The last time the High Witness saw him, he shared a bench with a Satanist.

They already knew the whole story—the Judge, and the High Witness. Both knew every word he planned for his defense; his entire argument was already taken into account. He no longer believed this trial was for him—it was for the crowd; they were giving the throng another moose to wave at. He was simply the attraction of the day.

The Judge waited as the seats filled; then as the people standing found their spots; and those looking on through the open doors to settle down. The sun shone brightly over the room. Despite all his bravery and notions about dignity, Ohj's shoulders hunched, and he couldn't lift his head. He twisted to look behind; the court spilled over with spectators— all focused on him. He remembered then, that he wore the red t-shirt with his old anti-leniency slogan printed on it. He faced forward again, shrinking down even further. How did he become the fool?

He wanted to stand up straight and face the Judge like the warrior he was, but his knees trembled too much to hold up his weight. His throat was swollen. No matter how hard he tried to look up, his eyes kept falling. On the floor to the right, he saw the sturdy pile of chains.

When the Judge addressed him, Ohj forced his knees to straighten and lock. He looked up into the frozen blue eyes and nodded his head.

"Ohj, you are charged with defying God, and with murder." The Judge's words were neither angry nor sympathetic. The quiet tone traveled easily across the hushed courtroom. "Both charges carry the sentence of complete and final banishment."

Tears started to gather in Ohj's eyes. This was his time to declare his innocence, demand consideration for leniency. He'd worded his arguments to perfection in the forest, repeating them in his head over, and over again, so that he wouldn't get caught speechless. He only needed to open his mouth and his defense would come pouring out.

Instead, he dropped to his knees.

Red put his hand on Ohj's shoulder. "Your Honor, we are begging for forgiveness. Ohj has served many lifetimes fighting for the cause of righteousness...."

Here was his, "good-guy" speech. Ohj had heard millions of them, given by guardians who loved their people and wanted desperately to save them. Ohj knew how it went. The speech would bring everyone to tears, and then it would be the witness' turn to tell the judge what a villain he really was.

Yes, he'd fought hard for centuries, and then worked centuries more bringing people to justice. But when it came down to it, all those years of goodness didn't excuse murder and treason.

The Judge nodded to the High Witness to begin his prosecution. The High Witness didn't hold stacks of thick accounts to read from—one very small blessing.

"Your Honor, Ohj is an esteemed witness, given great responsibility. He used that gift to betray God. Using the very sacred trust bestowed on him, he began to intervene instead of witnessing the crimes in his care. He used this power to commit murder, perjury and treason. If I may, I'd like to give a few details?" He didn't wait for permission. "In four of his interventions, Ohj outright killed a human. He killed without mercy. On another four occasions, his interventions resulted in a human's death. By hastening each individual's death, Ohj robbed them of the chance for redemption. If they had lived, each person might have turned from evil and repented, and saved themselves."

Red interrupted the High Witness. "Your Honor, I arbitrated over every one of those cases. I sentenced the first-time offenders lightly, if at all. The crimes committed by the rest designated the severity of their sentence." He kept his hand on Ohj's shoulder. "In all the cases, Ohj saved innocent lives."

"And in saving those few lives, he damned the souls of others," the High Witness spoke out. "Your Honor, that is the ultimate crime. Lastly, he was recruited to renounce God. The very fact that Ohj enticed such evil, tells the court that he doesn't belong amongst us."

Vincent—Ohj knew he had to come into this eventually.

"Ohj, do you have anything to say for yourself?" the Judge asked.

Ohj wanted to tell him about the little boy who cried for his mother as his tongue was about to be sliced off, and about the little girl being raped; or of the future victims, unknowingly lying in wait as the murderers finished their lifetime killing sprees. He meant to explain how the brutal killings finally got to him. How agonizing and terrible all the pain was.

Still on his knees, he lifted his head to the Judge. He found no more warmth or forgiveness in the pious eyes than before.

Ohj dropped his head back down. "I felt the victims' fear and pain. I could no longer turn my back."

The court remained quiet. His defense finished.

"Ohj, this court finds you guilty of murder and treason," the Judge began.

Ohj squeezed his eyes shut as the Judge continued with his sentence. He tucked his head down further.

"For your crimes, you will be taken from this court and cast out of heaven for all of eternity."

Then complete silence. It was over.

The Judge nodded at the captain to chain him up. The soldiers wasted no time. The tinny jangling woke up the crowd. They got to their feet with a roar. Ohj kept his eyes shut. He felt pressure on his shoulder as two of the soldiers held him down on his knees. They pulled his arms behind him and started winding the cold steel around his wrists. The weight held his arms immobile. It took three soldiers to help him to his feet. The soldiers hung onto his arms in case he tried to run, while another began to weave the chains around his ankles.

"You can't do this to him," Red cried out. He ran up to the podium. "He's not a criminal; you can't send him into a life of torment."

But he was a criminal, a perjurer, and a murderer. Ohj knew this himself.

Three witnesses ran to join Red in front of the Judge. As they begged him to reconsider, the Judge nodded at the soldiers to begin their exit. The captain tugged on Ohj's arm. Ohj tried to take a step, but the chains were wound too tightly around his ankles. He started to fall, but the soldiers braced him up. He tried a smaller step, then another, shuffling forward with the soldier's support on each side. He kept his eyes on his feet, determined not to fall. Two of the soldiers stood at the back of the entourage, facing the crowd.

The sky darkened. The change in light hushed the yelling. The soldiers stopped pulling Ohj along as everyone looked up. Storm clouds gathered above, gray and black- edged. Sparkles of light shifted within as the clouds began to roil. Ohj didn't look, too tired for a light show. Thunder pounded, vibrating the courtroom. A wind picked up. Ohj could feel it pulling on his shirt.

"He's to receive mercy," Red declared loudly over the storm.

Ohj finally lifted his head, afraid to hope.

"Bring him back," the Judge ordered the soldiers.

Ohj looked up at the Judge through the hair fallen over his eyes.

"Ohj, you are indeed being shown mercy. The Lord is going to spare you."

Ohj fell back on his knees. The courtroom went into a frenzy of cheering. Ohj felt both gratitude and shame, remembering how their exuberance used to irritate him. He shook his head, sighing, waiting for the Judge to set him free.

Red ran to his side and started to untangle the chains. "Get these off. Let him go."

Instead, the captain looked at the Judge.

The Judge shook his head, no. "Let me continue," he spoke above the noise. When the crowd quieted enough for him to be heard, he addressed Ohj directly. "You are no longer cast out. But because of the seriousness of your crimes, you must still face punishment. Your crimes will not be tolerated or ignored."

Ohj lifted himself as far as he could and strained forward to hear the next words.

"You are sentenced to eternity in prison. Now go."

"Wait," Red yelled. "He's been shown mercy."

"Yes, he most certainly has. Take him now," the Judge told the captain. "His trial is over."

"What does that mean?" Ohj asked Red.

Red didn't answer, still staring at the Judge.

The soldiers hoisted him back to his feet. The captain tugged on his arm to lead him away again. He'd heard scattered talk of a prison, but since it didn't concern him, never paid much attention.

"Red, I don't understand."

Red walked beside him. "This sentence is just as permanent. No one is ever released from prison. My guess is you will never again see the light of day. You will never have another soul to talk to. You will be forever separated from God and everything good. The merciful part is, you'll also be separated from everything evil."

As Ohj shuffled between the two soldiers, guardians began weeping. Red followed their painfully slow progress. They headed toward the same hallway they carried Vincent and all the other damned souls. Ohj started to panic, trying to breathe while they moved him ahead. He only remembered one hallway, the one that led to the wrought iron gates. Was that the prison he now faced—the hitching post? He thought he'd escaped that fate.

He started to pull back. "Wait, I don't understand."

The soldiers lifted him off his feet to continue forward. He started bucking as the entourage headed through the double doors. "Red, stop them."

It took every one of the soldiers to carry him as he twisted and kicked. Blinded with fear, he didn't notice the terrible smell, or feel his arm tearing.

"You don't understand what they're going to do to me," he screamed at the soldiers. "What I'll become there—this is worse than torture. Please, God. Wait."

Instead of passing through the wrought iron gates, they carried him off to the side. Ohj shifted his eyes when they turned down this new hallway. He stopped fighting. His head dropped back, and he watched as the wrought iron gates got further and further away. The soldiers put him back down on his feet.

They shuffled past doorway after doorway. With every curve of the hallway, the walls grew darker. The doors on either side were held shut by wide strips of steel, bolted on with thick rivets. The rusted bolts warned Ohj that once tightened, they were forgotten. No sound came from behind the doors, at least

208

nothing that could be heard above his chains. He began to understand what this new mercy entailed. He tried to swallow, but his raw throat wouldn't respond.

They came to a stop in front of an open door. The captain unlocked Ohj's chains. The ground shook when they fell off.

"I'm afraid you have to strip down," he told Ohj.

Ohj pulled his red t-shirt over his head with one arm; his infected arm useless. He took off his pants and shoes the same way. He then stood in front of the soldiers, cold, with nothing to hide his damaged skin and shrunken muscles. Red looked away.

Ohj blinked to stop the tears from shaming him even more.

"Wait," Red reached into his pocket. "I have something for you." He handed Ohj a pack of cigarettes.

Menthol. Ohj attempted a smile. Red reached into another pocket for a book of matches.

"I don't know about this," the captain said. "We're stripping him down, how can I justify all that mess?"

Red shoved the matches into Ohj's hand. "There aren't even enough to light the whole pack. "What's he gonna do, burn the door down?"

"All right. Go on in, now," the captain pointed at the doorway.

Ohj looked inside. It was completely dark, except for the little sliver of light from the hallway. He stepped forward and almost tripped, not expecting the two-foot drop to the floor. He hung onto the doorway and stepped down. Before the door shut behind him, he looked around his new home. No lamp, so no possibility of light. The plot was minuscule. Unless the dark corners were bigger than they looked. No padding to soften the walls or the floor. There wasn't a cot or a chair to sit on, or even a sink to wash his face.

He turned and looked up at Red. "I can do this. Don't worry about me."

The captain shut the door. Complete darkness rushed in at him. The door had no knob on the inside, confirming that he was never going to open it. He wished he'd gotten the chance to wash first. Had he thought of it, he would have requested a bowl of water before they closed him in for all of eternity.

He took out a cigarette as he listened to the clanging sounds of the door getting bolted. He struck a match; only fifteen more to go. As he took his first puffs, they finished securing the door. He leaned against it to feel the last vibrations, to hear any voices.

Too soon, everything stilled.

Ohj took another puff, his exhale loud in the tiny space. He really could do this. How often had he wished he could be alone? Granted he'd like a little light and fresh water, but he'd have to make do. He used one cigarette to light another, and then used the red, lit end to explore his new home. He didn't have to go far, maybe three steps in each direction.

He walked around in a circle then sat down on the ground. Red would work on his behalf. Red wouldn't forget him. How could he, with his courtroom just down the hall—albeit a very long hall. They had taken so many turns; Ohj wasn't sure if they'd stayed in the same building or were in some grim, underground dungeon. Still, Red would try to get him an appeal, or at least get him moved to somewhere with a window.

He seemed to doze off, he couldn't tell. He stood up when his legs started to tingle. He lit another smoke and walked around in a circle, inhaling and exhaling. How long would the cigarettes last him at this rate? He should try to ration them to one every thousand years. But he needed the action now, the purpose of movement, so he again used one to light another. Eventually, he'd probably go insane anyway. Better to calm himself now.

"Hey, anyone there? Anyone hear me?" He felt for the crevice to the door. "Red, thanks for the smokes, but don't suppose I could get a window." Leaning against the door, he took another puff.

How could he have been so stupid? Of course, they didn't arrest him after Wayne. They didn't have to—his body had already started a punishing, slow death. His body itself set the motion; didn't need the soldiers to make it official. Arresting him was one thing, but why didn't they stop him? Vincent and his friends knew what he was doing. The High Court knew, but still they allowed him to keep intervening and/or murder people. That is, until he couldn't do it anymore, Ohj thought wryly.

They locked him away the minute he became useless. He tried to walk another circle but kept banging into a wall. He realized he no longer held the pack of menthols. He got down and felt around blindly on the floor. He found the matches and struck one to find the pack. Holding the burning match in front, he went for the pack where it had been kicked into the corner. The match burnt out before his shaking fingers could pull out a cigarette. Once he got one lit, he smoked the rest of the pack, lighting one off the other. He cupped each cigarette inside his palm, close to his chest to get the heat off the burning end.

He ended up flat on the floor again with his feet propped up by a wall. Dazed, he sat up. His bad arm was completely dead, hanging onto his body without being an actual part of it. He tried to rub some circulation back into it. How long had he been in there? Days? Years? He leaned against the wall to listen for any noise. He pounded a few times, hoping some lost soul on the other side responded.

Then he pounded again. "Hey, in there. Hey, if we band together, they can't ignore us," he shouted to his prison mates. "If we make enough noise, they'll have to come see what's going on."

Nothing.

"A little effort on all our parts would be worth a try." Going from wall to wall, he kept pounding and shouting. "Maybe they'll toss us a flashlight."

He turned but seemed to hit the opposite wall immediately. He struck one of his last matches to light up the area around him. The plot seemed smaller. He sat down on the floor with his knees up to his chest, holding them tight to stop the shivering. He closed his eyes but wasn't sure if they were really closed or not.

He tried to picture the lake, and imagine himself near the water, feeling the sun on his face. He listened for the birds and silly babble of the guardians. In his mind, he sat on grass, his body molded perfectly into the hill. When his fingers touched cold, hard floor, not velvety blades, he started to cry.

The space didn't allow enough room for him to stretch his legs, so he couldn't stay down for long.

He'd lost the book of matches. When he put his hand out to try to find them, his fingers hit a wall, bending back his nails. The area seemed so much smaller. He shook out his hand, and reached out again, immediately hitting the other wall. The walls seemed to close in on him. Already he'd begun to lose his mind. Way too soon for him to go insane.

Now unable to find the door, he started banging on wall behind him.

"Anybody there?" His voice hollered back at him, hurting his ears.

He got down to feel around again for the matches, panicking as he hit one corner after another. He stood up, backing against a wall. He couldn't raise his hand to his face. He turned, thinking he must have worked his way into a corner.

He could feel the walls on all sides of him tightening, until he could no longer bend his knees to crouch down. He pounded his fist on the wall in front of him.

"Help. Someone. Something's wrong," he yelled out. He pushed on the wall in front of him as it pressed in on his chest, crushing him. He used his back to brace himself, but still the walls shifted inward, imploding the room, wedging every inch of his flesh.

"I'm dying in here. Someone, please, I'm dying in here." He screamed. "God, help me, please."

As he was squeezed beyond endurance, his mouth opened to scream again. With no breath to fuel the effort, his cries were inaudible. "God, I can't breathe," he mouthed.

The light blinded him.

He screamed out in shock when a burst of air hit his lungs and bare skin.

A man held him up. "Julia, you have a healthy, baby boy."

Ohj cringed at the assault. He seemed to be tossed around in the air, until finally dropped on a hard surface. Hands were all over him, rubbing his skin, stretching his legs, pushing on his knees. He tried to pull himself free. Keeping his eyes shut tight against the hot light, he flailed his fists blindly. A woman shoved something inside his nose, sucking out the air he so desperately tried to inhale.

When he screamed at the woman to stop, he saw her. Just over the woman's shoulder—Asia. She stood behind the woman and looked down on him. She smiled faintly. He stopped fighting.

The human forced one of his eyelids apart to squirt a gel in. He screamed a protest, recoiling, while trying to keep his focus on Asia. With his one good eye, he caught sight of the Judge from the High Court: the being who had just sent him to this prison. The Judge stood in the corner of the room, so tall his head brushed the ceiling. He burned brighter than the fluorescent lights. Another being stood beside him, a birthing witness, watching calmly as Ohj alone struggled to defend himself.

Ohj reached out to them, needing answers. The human next shoved her fingers into his good eye, squirting in more ointment. The entire room blurred. He yelled out. Ignoring his objection, the woman rolled him on his stomach first, then back again, inside a fabric. The tight fabric pinned his arms down, until he was helpless.

He tried to focus on Asia as he flew through the air again, back into the man's arms.

"Everything's perfect. His scores are good. And he is one very strong baby. You have a fighter on your hands," the man said. "And this is a remarkable birthmark on his arm."

The man tore the blanket away from Ohj's shoulder to expose his infected arm.

"From my angle, it looks kind of like a little sword. Very interesting."

The human handed the bundle over to a woman in bed. She pulled Ohj's face up close to dry lips and kissed him. Ohj tried to look around her to find Asia, buried within the sea of people in the room. He blinked madly against the goop, looking for her long, strawberry-brown hair.

Asia walked over to stand in front a human, blocking Ohj's vision of teddy bear scrubs. Her smile was gone. She shook out wide, pearly sleeves to create a barricade around them.

"Get some rest. We have work to do."

The beautiful angel put her hand on top of Ohj's head and smoothed back the damp, downy fuzz. "It's time to fight."

Despite all his effort, his eyes closed.

Ohj fell asleep.